BIONICLE

Challenge
of the Hordika

BIONICLE®

FIND THE POWER,
LIVE THE LEGEND

The legend comes alive in these exciting BIONICLE® books:

BIONICLE®

Challenge
of the Hordika

by Greg Farshtey

SCHOLASTIC INC.
New York Toronto London Auckland Sydney
Mexico City New Delhi Hong Kong Buenos Aires

ISBN 0-439-69621-6

12 11 10 9 8 7 6 5 4 3 2   5 6 7 8 9/0

Printed in the U.S.A.
First printing, April 2005

For Justin and Daniel,
makers of monsters

INTRODUCTION

Turaga Vakama knelt before the Amaja Circle. Before him sat the six Toa Nuva, Takanuva, and Hahli, the Matoran currently serving as Chronicler. All of them were waiting for him to continue a story he dreaded having to tell.

"You know, not long after the Matoran came to this island of Mata Nui, their memories of the past disappeared," he began. "All that had happened in the city of Metru Nui, the good and the bad, was lost to them. Sometimes . . . sometimes I think they were most fortunate in that regard."

Hahli looked down at the tablet on which she was carving Vakama's words. She had never heard the Turaga sound so defeated, as if the weight of a thousand years was on his shoulders.

She could not imagine what happened in Metru Nui that could so affect him. For the first time, she found herself wishing someone else was the Chronicler.

"We had escaped Metru Nui, we six Toa Metru, with a small number of Matoran. Each of them was locked in a deep sleep, induced by Makuta as part of his grand scheme of conquest. We had found a new land — this land — where the Matoran would be safe. Now we had only to return to the quake-ravaged city and recover them all."

Vakama scattered a number of small black stones in the sandpit. "What we could not know was that, in our absence, the city had been seized by the spider creatures called Visorak. Due to our . . . *my* . . . overconfidence, we were captured shortly after we returned there. Trapped in cocoons, we were mutated by Visorak venom into half Toa, half beasts called Toa Hordika. Only the actions of six strangers, the Rahaga, saved us from death."

The Turaga's voice dropped to a whisper. "Better we had perished . . . that is what some of us thought at the time. The Rahaga told us we must find a cure for our condition within a limited time, or risk remaining as Hordika — or worse — for all eternity. Instead, we chose to focus our efforts on saving the Matoran, worrying about ourselves when they were safe.

"It was a difficult decision. The rage of the Rahi ruled our hearts, and in none more than mine. We faced enemies of great power and great cunning, and we had to do it stripped of our mask powers, stripped of our traditional Toa tools, yes, stripped of our very selves. . . ."

Roodaka, viceroy of the Visorak hordes, stood in what had once been Turaga Dume's box in the Coliseum. A red Visorak, Vohtarak, stood beside her, awaiting her commands. Down below, Visorak scurried to and fro, carrying cocooned Rahi. These would be placed in the webs that lined the arena as trophies of another conquest.

Soon, the Toa would be joining them, she knew. The six heroes of Metru Nui had combined their powers to trap their foe, Makuta, in a protodermis prison sealed with the symbol of the three Matoran virtues: unity, duty, and destiny. With such a "lock," even Makuta could not break free. Only the power of the Toa could undo what they had done.

"Vakama and his allies made two great errors," Roodaka said. "The first was thinking Makuta helpless. Though his body is frozen, though his power is stalemated, his mind is free to roam. His thoughts reached out to us and now Metru Nui is ours."

The Vohtarak nodded agreement enthusiastically. Not agreeing with Roodaka was almost inevitably a fatal mistake.

Roodaka smiled as she recalled the Toa's return to Metru Nui. So proud they were, so confident, so convinced that nothing could defeat them. But the venom of the Visorak changed all that. Now the Toa were Toa Hordika, half-hero, half-Rahi, forced for the first time to confront the shadows within.

"They should have fled far from this place," Roodaka reflected. "They should have traveled to a star of which even Mata Nui never dreamed. Now there is no hope for them. In a matter of hours, days at most, the hordes will track them down."

Roodaka glanced at the Vohtarak. "But why am I telling you this? You are not even a Visorak . . . are you?"

The Vohtarak hesitated for a moment under Roodaka's piercing glare. Then, with a shrug, the Visorak transformed into a perfect replica of Toa Nokama.

"Once again, you are correct." The voice was Nokama's, but the Toa of Water had never worn such an expression of hatred. "I am Krahka. I am a Rahi, one of those your hordes have been hunting in this city. And I have come to strike you down like the monster you are."

Roodaka's answer was laughter, long and shrill, carrying with it more than a little trace of madness.

Krahka circled warily. The shapeshifting Rahi had faced many foes in her life, including the six Toa Metru. But this Roodaka was something different. Every move she made was carefully calculated and all part of a grand strategy. There was no wasted motion, no scrambling to react to Krahka's changes of shape.

For her part, Roodaka was enjoying this. She could have had Krahka slain immediately, but chose instead to face the Rahi in single battle. The arena floor had been cleared for them. Now the Visorak watched as their leader prepared to claim another victim.

Krahka had abandoned the guise of Nokama in favor of a subterranean creature whose appearance would be enough to drive a sane Matoran mad. She now towered twelve feet high, with a slimy, pale white body and six long, bony spines coming out of her sides. Each spine was extremely flexible and could be cracked like a whip. At the end of the spines were wickedly curved claws that could rip through six inches of metal with one swipe.

It should have been no contest. The Krahka had strength, height, and reach over Roodaka, and a body designed to make it impossible for any blow to land solidly. But the Visorak viceroy slipped away from every one of Krahka's strikes, then struck with her own talons. Worse, Roodaka struck so swiftly and so often that Krahka had no opportunity to shapeshift.

Roodaka slipped through her defenses and landed two quick blows, staggering her opponent. Then she launched her Rhotuka spinner, whose power could transform Krahka permanently into a figure out of nightmare. At the last split second, the Rahi shifted into a small burrowing creature and vanished underground.

Silence descended on the arena. Some of the Visorak believed Roodaka had won, while others were not so certain. Roodaka herself stood perfectly still, waiting for Krahka's return in a new form.

The ground shifted slightly beneath the Visorak viceroy's feet. Before she could react, the arena floor was crumbling beneath her and she was falling into the massive, tooth-filled maw of a Po-Metru troller worm. Some of the horde charged forward as if to save her, while the rest seemed perfectly happy to see Roodaka devoured.

They were destined to be disappointed. Roodaka latched onto the sides of the hole with her claws and pulled herself out right before the huge jaws snapped shut. Once back on solid ground, she paused and listened to the sound of the great worm moving beneath the surface.

Moving too quickly for the eye to follow, Roodaka plunged her arm through the ground and seized the Krahka/troller in her claws. With a mighty heave, she pulled the giant worm up through the arena floor.

As soon as she realized her predicament, Krahka shifted to a smaller lava eel. Her now fiery hot hide burnt Roodaka's hand, forcing her to release her grip. Krahka slithered away and shifted again, this time taking the form of one of the gigantic Kahgarak spiders that guarded the gates of the Coliseum. Then she spat a stream of webbing at Roodaka, binding her to the arena wall.

"You . . . cannot defeat me . . . with my own creatures," Roodaka hissed. Flexing her muscles, she tore free of the web. "And at that size, you are too big of a target to miss, Rahi."

Roodaka launched another spinner. Krahka started to shapeshift, but too late as the whirling energy struck her. The Rahi's own powers blunted the effects of the mutating force, but it was still enough to send her sprawling in the dust. Now back in the form of Nokama, she struggled to regain her feet.

The Visorak viceroy was upon her before she could rise, a talon held to Krahka's throat. "I could end this now," said Roodaka. "But you have . . . possibilities, creature. I did not get where I am by wasting potential resources."

Krahka cursed. Roodaka grabbed her by the neck and forced her to look around the arena at the hundreds of Visorak assembled to watch the match. "At a single word from me, even a nod, they would bind you and turn you into something so horrible you would die of fright at your own reflection," said Roodaka. "Or we can come to an arrangement. You decide."

Roodaka let the Krahka go. The Rahi got to her feet, still in the shape of the Toa Metru of Water. "What sort of . . . arrangement?"

"Not every Rahi need end up in our web, Krahka. Those who are useful will survive intact, even thrive, under my rule. You can be one of them. Your particular skills and your past experience with the Toa Metru — oh yes, I know about that — make you ideal for something I have in mind."

Krahka pondered the offer. If she refused, she had no doubt that Roodaka and the Visorak would defeat her . . . or worse. If she accepted, there might still be some opportunity to get her revenge on Roodaka later on.

"All right," said the Rahi. "Very well. What do you want me to do?"

Roodaka smiled. "Sidorak and the hordes are hunting for the Toa Hordika. If they catch them, all is well; but just in case they do not, I intend to make sure that the Toa will be unable to oppose me."

"How?"

Roodaka put an arm around Krahka's shoulders and led her away. "We are going to do the heroes of Metru Nui a favor, you and I. We are going to tell them the truth about themselves."

"I want the truth," said Nuju. "What are we doing here?"

He was standing on the outskirts of Ko-Metru, a district devastated by earthquake and overrun with Visorak spiders. The crystal surface of a Knowledge Tower reflected his distorted appearance. Once a powerful Toa, the venom of the Visorak had transformed Nuju and his friends into monstrous Toa Hordika.

Nuju studied his reflection. His mask and tools had been warped beyond all recognition. His body was stronger, but twisted like that of a Rahi. Worse than that were the changes he felt inside. The Toa and beast halves of his mind were at war now. It took all his willpower to fight down the animalistic rage that threatened to consume him.

He turned to see that Rahaga Kualus was not listening to him. The small, bizarre figure's eyes were trained on the sky. Nuju followed his gaze and saw nothing but the occasional ice bat swooping across the sky.

"Beautiful, aren't they?" Kualus whispered. "Perfectly aerodynamic. Completely efficient distribution of mass. And their flight speed — did you know that an ice bat can outrace a stampeding Kikanalo herd?"

"No," Nuju replied coldly. "I did not."

The Toa Hordika wished he could just walk away and leave this strange little being to his obvious obsession with flying creatures. But circumstances dictated that he could not. There was a mission to perform and he needed Kualus' help to complete it.

"We are wasting time," growled Nuju. "We have a city of sleeping Matoran to save. We came here to salvage parts needed to build transport, not to admire birds."

"Rodents," said Kualus. "Ice bats are rodents. Surprised a scholar like you wouldn't know that. What were you looking at all those years in the observatory?"

The Rahaga pointed toward a lone bat flying shakily toward the ground. Its wing had been damaged in a collision with a Knowledge Tower. Unable to control its flight, it was headed straight for a Visorak web.

"Stay here," Kualus said, already leaping over rubble to follow the ice bat.

"What are you doing?" said Nuju. "It's just a bi . . . a rodent!"

"I am doing the same thing Toa do," replied Kualus. "I am saving one who cannot save himself."

Keen eyes tracking the bat's flight path, Kualus unleashed the spinner attached to his back. It flew straight and true through the air until it reached the bat. The spinner immediately adhered to the flesh of the flyer and steered it back toward the waiting Rahaga. Kualus snagged the spinner and removed the wounded creature from it. Then he began to gently tend the Rahi's wounds.

"Handy little thing, isn't it?" said Kualus. "They are called Rhotuka spinners."

"Yes," said Nuju. "If I ever need a bat catcher, you are the first one I'll call."

Kualus hastily improvised a splint for the bat's wing. Once he was done, he placed the creature inside a niche in a damaged Knowledge Tower. When the ice bat tried to leave the shelter, the Rahaga began talking to the Rahi in clicks and whistles, all the while making sharp gestures with his hands. What was even more amazing was that the ice bat seemed to be listening.

"What is that gibberish?" asked Nuju, his impatience growing by the moment.

"Not gibberish," Kualus replied, smiling. "Language — the language of the flyers, or at least as close to it as a non-flyer can come. Just as they don't waste any energy when in the air, they don't waste words when they speak. Perhaps you might like to learn?"

Nuju shook his head. "No. Now can we move on?"

Kualus sprang to his feet. "Very well, Toa Hordika. Lead, and I shall follow . . . as long as I like where you are leading."

*   *   *

Toa Hordika Nokama and Rahaga Gaaki swam silently along the eastern coast of Metru Nui. All along the shoreline, Gaaki could see Visorak Boggarak webbing up the sea creatures they had captured. Some of the unfortunate captives would be mutated by venom, the rest simply condemned to endless sleep.

Nokama had taken no notice. She was at one with the ocean, moving through the water with strong, smooth strokes. It seemed that she could sense every movement in the water, from small currents and eddies to the passage of even the tiniest fish. Sensing the approach of swells, she let her body go limp and rode with them. She had never known such complete peace, certainly not since she had become a Toa Metru. It seemed strange that such a monstrous mutation as becoming a Hordika could bring such a feeling.

"No. It is not all bad," said Gaaki. "Allowing the animal to guide you can be so tempting, you might never wish to turn back."

"Would that be so terrible?" asked Nokama. "I can still serve my city. I can still protect the Matoran . . . even like this."

"But can you protect your friends? Can you protect yourself?" asked Gaaki. "It takes a being of great willpower not to succumb to the lure of the Hordika. Yes, you may discover new powers and new ways of being, but you may also revert to a primal state and bring destruction to everything you hold dear."

Nokama wished the Rahaga would just shut up. She was not going to destroy anything — the very thought was absurd. Instead, she was going to use her new abilities to be an even better protector of Metru Nui than before.

Gaaki was just jealous, she decided. Even in this form, Nokama was lithe and strong. Of course, Gaaki envied her that.

I shall let her remain by my side, thought Nokama. *But I shall keep an eye on this one. I do not know that I trust her.*

*　　*　　*

High above Le-Metru, a member of the Visorak Roparak species kept a careful watch. Its brown coloration allowed it to fade into the tangled mass of cables and webbing that shrouded the Metru. Beside it, an unfortunate Gukko bird tried in vain to escape a cocoon. The creature would fail, of course, and soon cease to be any threat.

The Roparak had to forego the pleasure of watching its captive's struggles. The green Toa and his companion, the Rahaga named Iruini, had appeared only moments before. Their behavior was puzzling, to say the least. The Rahaga traveled rapidly over the rubble, but constantly had to stop and urge the Toa on. The Roparak could not understand everything that was being said, of course, since Visorak knowledge of the Matoran language was rudimentary at best. But it could recognize the tone. It was the same tone that the viceroy of the Visorak, Roodaka, got in her voice just before she dropped one of her guards from a high place.

The Roparak had already sent a message through the webs to let others know the Toa was here. Since their escape from the Coliseum, the six Toa Hordika had been on the run. They had so far managed to evade a few halfhearted efforts by the Visorak to catch them, and no doubt thought they were superior to the hordes. Little did they realize the spiders were simply testing their defenses before beginning the hunt in earnest.

Nearby, the Gukko bird had finally exhausted itself and given up. In a short while, it would be locked in sleep, with no more worries, cares, dreams, or desires. Its system would slow to such a point that nutrition would no longer be required. There would no longer be any need to seek food, or fly over the city, or build a nest in the cables. The Roparak wondered what such complete isolation from the world would be like. The idea of having no Roodaka to answer to was strangely appealing.

The Visorak caught itself just in time. True, Roodaka couldn't read its thoughts — hopefully — but the dark one she served . . . that one knew all. It was best to concentrate on the hunt, and not risk thinking thoughts that could lead to an early end to existence.

The Toa and the Rahaga had vanished inside of the large buildings. The Visorak had no idea what they were seeking there, but it really did not matter. Vibrations in the web indicated that the horde was closing in.

The first Toa to fall would serve as bait for the rest. The heroes would walk right into the center of a web . . . and never walk out again.

"This was your idea," said Iruini. "Now you are having second thoughts."

"Third and fourth," replied Matau. "Thank you for spot-noticing."

The Toa cleared away some rubble that blocked their path. The Rahaga was right. It had been Matau's suggestion that the Toa use airships to transport the Matoran out safely. But the Visorak had wrecked all the existing vessels in Le-Metru, which meant building more. The Toa had split up to find the necessary materials and anything of importance they might need to bring on the journey. Odds were that if — *when*, Matau corrected — the Matoran were rescued, there would be precious little time to load the ships and go. They had come to this airship hangar in search of undamaged protodermis membranes that could be used for new vessels.

"What would you rather be doing?" asked Iruini.

"Finding that Rahi you spoke of," said Matau. "Keetongu — the one who can cure me of . . . this."

Iruini snorted. "I suppose you still believe that Mata Nui comes through the chutes on Naming Day bringing gifts to good Matoran, too. Keetongu is a myth, Matau. Some of the other Rahaga believe in him, but I don't. A Rahi as big as that existing for so long without being found? Please."

"Oh," said Matau. "Then there's no hope? We will remain Hordika forever?"

Iruini ran, leapt, grabbed an overhanging pipe and did some lightning fast gymnastics. Then he let go, somersaulting three times in midair before landing on his feet. "It's not so bad. You get used to it."

Matau looked at the Rahaga in surprise. "You mean you —?"

Iruini crouched atop a pile of rubble and smiled. "Do you think I always looked like this? Did you think my name was always Rahaga Iruini? Not so." The Rahaga jumped to the ground, rolled, and sprang up again in front of Matau. "Toa Iruini, it was, once . . . long ago. But you never forget, brother. Trust me, you never forget."

Toa Hordika Onewa and Pouks crouched atop a canyon wall. Down below, a small herd of Kane-Ra bulls stirred uneasily in front of a cavern entrance. With all the Po-Matoran gone, the herd had staked out this area as their own territory. They had already been forced to defend it against Muaka cats and so were alert and on edge.

"All right," said Pouks. "Half a dozen Kane-Ra between you and your goal, Onewa. What's the plan?"

"That's easy. I use my Kanohi Mask of Mind Control on the herd leader and make them stampede."

Pouks shook his head. "Masks don't work for Hordika, carver. Try again."

Onewa shrugged, obviously annoyed. "Then I use my power over stone. I cause a rockslide and scare them off."

"Better. Not good, but better." Pouks' tone was mocking. "Got another guess?"

Onewa stood up and tore a chunk of rock out of the canyon wall. "I take this boulder and I throw it at them," he shouted. "And I keep throwing more until they are buried underneath them. I might even save one for you, Rahaga, if you don't shut up. Then I march over the Kane-Ra and I get what I came for!"

Pouks walked over and put a hand on Onewa's arm. He exerted a gentle pressure, trying to get the Toa to drop the rock, but Onewa continued to hold it aloft. "That's the Hordika part of you talking," said Pouks. "That's the part that wants to hurt and destroy."

The Rahaga pointed down into the canyon. Two Kane-Ra were charging each other, heads lowered and sharp horns primed to pierce each others' flanks. "You can overcome that part of you, Toa, or you can end up no better than them."

Glaring at the Rahaga, Onewa lifted the rock a little higher. Pouks looked into his eyes, searching for some sign that a hero of Metru Nui still lived inside that monstrous shell. *If the Hordika side has already taken over, I am in for a disappointment*, he said to himself. *A crushing disappointment.*

Since becoming a Toa, Whenua had been in a number of strange places and situations. After being transformed into a bestial Hordika, he fully expected to be in even more bizarre settings. But somehow he had never pictured himself lying half-buried in dirt outside an Archives entrance.

"What exactly are we doing?" he asked.

The Rahaga named Bomonga said nothing. He didn't even turn to look at the Toa.

"We are supposed to be gathering levitation disks," Whenua tried again. "Remember?"

This time, Bomonga glanced at his companion. Then he went back to staring into the darkness.

"What are we looking for?" Whenua asked, irritated. "And why are we doing it from under a pile of dirt?"

Bomonga's answer was more silence.

Whenua started to get up. The Rahaga grabbed his wrist and, showing surprising strength, yanked him back down to the ground. "Hey!" snapped Whenua.

The Rahaga pointed into the darkness. An instant later, a night creeper came scurrying across the broken pavement. Roughly seven feet long, with six powerful legs, the creeper's jaws snapped open and shut as it hunted through the rubble for food.

Whenua was about to say something about there being a time and a place for Rahi watching when something else entered the scene. It was a black Visorak spider crawling rapidly toward the creeper. When the nocturnal Rahi realized its danger, it was already too late. The Visorak spat a stream of webbing, entangling the creeper.

Bomonga's eyes narrowed. With a guttural snarl, he launched his spinner. The whirling disk flew silently through the air to strike the Visorak and adhere to its body. The spider froze in place. Without waiting for Whenua, the Rahaga sprang from the dirt and began tearing at the webbing that bound the creeper.

By the time the Toa reached the spot, the Rahi was already free. It raced off into the night without a backward glance. Bomonga gestured toward the Visorak, which still stood like a Po-Metru statue. "Learn," said the Rahaga.

The Hordika part of Whenua rebelled at getting too close to the Visorak. It was an instinctive revulsion, one which took all of the Toa's willpower to overcome. He reminded himself that before becoming a Toa or a Hordika, he had been an archivist. This was a chance to study the enemy.

Somewhere in the night, a rock raptor howled. Whenua paused, listening to the mournful sound. He wanted to be out there in the shadows, too, exploring, hunting, fighting for survival. A Rahi had no responsibilities, no duties or obligations to others. The more he thought about it, the more that sounded like the right way to live.

He took a step away from the Visorak, then another, as if being pulled by a magnetic force. Bomonga vaulted over a slab of rock and put himself in Whenua's path. "Learn!" said the Rahaga.

"But —"

Bomonga shook his head, saying, "You learn, you survive. You don't . . . ?"

Reluctantly, Whenua turned back to the Visorak. But in his heart he knew it would not be long before he would be unable to resist the urge to join the Rahi prowling the city. When that time came, no Rahaga would be able to stop him.

Vakama smashed open the door to his old forge. He kept pounding on it long after the lock had given way, until the metal was dented and misshapen beyond repair. Then he looked around for something else to hit.

"Was that necessary?" asked Norik.

"No. But it was fun," answered Vakama. "Didn't you think so?"

Norik followed Vakama into the darkened

chamber. "All I saw was destruction with no purpose."

"So? I'm a Toa. All we do is destroy, didn't you know that? Our friendships, our homes, our city . . . all just rubble. We save no one, nothing, Rahaga. Not even ourselves."

Vakama picked up a handful of mask making tools and dashed them against the wall. "This place is full of useless junk," he growled. "We shouldn't have come back here."

"You spent many happy days here, did you not?" asked Norik. "Even after you became a Toa, you sometimes wished that you could go back to being a mask maker again, right here."

"I did a lot of stupid things when I was a Toa. That was the least of them."

"Anger rules your spirit, Vakama. It makes the burden of responsibility that you bear that much heavier, I know."

Vakama whirled, seized Norik, and lifted him into the air. "You don't know anything, little one! You don't know me. You don't know anything about me. So stop pretending you do!"

For a moment, Norik thought Vakama would strike him. But the Toa Hordika simply shrugged and dropped the Rahaga as if he were a broken mask. "Stay out of my way until this is finished," Vakama warned. "Or I won't be responsible for what happens to you."

"I can take care of myself," Norik answered, brushing himself off. "Can you say the same?"

Vakama didn't answer. Instead, he began rummaging through a pile of tools, half-finished items, broken masks, and other remnants of his past life. "I know they're here. Where are they?"

Norik watched him search, noting how casually he threw things aside that must have once had meaning for him. From what the others said, Vakama had always been the most driven of the Toa Metru. Now it seemed that trait was causing him to succumb to his Hordika side that much faster.

"What are you looking for?" the Rahaga asked. "Maybe I can help find it."

"Just before Lhikan was captured, I had gotten an order from Le-Metru for a half dozen sets of airship controls. I made the parts, but I never had the chance to send them out for assembly. They should still be here."

Vakama searched his work table and a few other piles on the floor, all without success. Frustrated, he picked up a Kanoka disk and hurled it across the room. It struck the wall, the impact triggering the disk's *weakness* power. The outer surface of the wall crumbled away, revealing a small compartment.

One glance at Vakama told Norik that the Toa Hordika had not been expecting this. He made it across the room in three quick strides and tore the hatch off the hidden compartment. He reached inside and emerged holding a fiery red Kanoka disk with the image of a Kanohi mask engraved upon it.

Vakama looked down at the disk as if it were a Lohrak serpent ready to bite him. "This makes no sense," he muttered. "None. It's not possible."

Norik climbed up the pipes and hovered over Vakama's shoulder. The mask depicted on the disk was definitely not the Toa Hordika's, nor did it belong to any of the other Toa. "What is this disk?"

Vakama raised the disk and slammed it against the ground. Fire erupted from the Kanoka. Toa Hordika and Rahaga watched it burn out in silence.

When Vakama finally spoke, he sounded like a lost being. "I don't understand. This is a Toa disk, Norik, for a Toa of Fire. It's like the one I found in the suva the day I became a Toa Metru. It had an image of my Mask of Concealment engraved upon it, a sign that I was destined to be a Toa by the will of Mata Nui."

The Toa Hordika picked up the still hot disk. "The mask on this Toa disk belongs to Nuhrii, a Ta-Matoran. He found one of the six Great Disks and helped us save Metru Nui from the Morbuzakh plant."

Vakama dug into his pack and pulled out his own Toa disk. Even though he no longer had his launcher, he still carried the disk as a symbol of what used to be. Now he looked at it as if seeing it for the very first time. Even from his high perch, Norik could see that something was very wrong.

"Something has been scratched out," Vakama said quietly. "I never noticed it before. Something was here and it was wiped away . . . and my mask carved on top of it."

The Toa Hordika slumped to the floor. "Can't you see? If all this is what it seems to be then it was Nuhrii's destiny all along. I am a . . . mistake. I was never meant to be Toa of Fire!"

Norik struggled to find words of comfort, but none came. He wanted to tell Vakama that there was some error, that this interpretation of the evidence must be mistaken. Instead, he said nothing. Silence, he decided, would be far better than lying.

Nokama and Gaaki approached a rear entrance of the Great Temple. They had been expecting numerous Visorak patrols to be guarding the place, but to their surprise, there were none. Even more amazing, the temple was largely intact.

The Toa Hordika opened the door and hesitated. Finally, she took a step forward, only to stop again. "What's the matter with me? Why does this feel wrong?"

"Because you are no longer wholly connected to Mata Nui," Gaaki said softly. "The Hordika side of you is a corruption. That's the same reason Visorak prefer to avoid places like this. Mata Nui is a spirit of creation, while they are creatures of destruction."

"We will need the Great and Noble Masks stored in here when we return to the island,"

Nokama replied. "So my Toa half will just have to be stronger."

Steeling herself, she took a step into the darkness of the temple, then another, and another. None of them got any easier. She made straight for the special chamber in which Kanohi masks were stored following their creation in Ta-Metru. The faster she got what she came for and got out of here, the happier she would be.

Nokama tore the lock off the outer door to the chamber and opened it wide. She stopped dead at the sight that greeted her. A small creature, perhaps a foot and a half in height, stood between her and the inner door. It regarded her quizzically, but did not seem to pose any threat. Still, when she sidestepped, it moved with her to block her advance. By the third time this happened, Nokama had lost patience.

"Stand aside!" the Toa Hordika snapped.

By this time, Gaaki had caught up with Nokama. "Who is that?" the Rahaga asked.

"I don't know. It seems to be guarding this place. But why against me?"

"It is no Matoran, or Matoran creation," Gaaki said with certainty. "It is a creature that should not exist."

Nokama went down to one knee to be on eye level with the guardian. "Listen to me. I am Toa Nokama, the Toa Metru of Water. I need the masks inside that chamber. You have to let me in for the sake of the city."

The little figure looked at her intently. It was almost comical in appearance, but she was in no mood to laugh. It flicked out its foot as if to kick away a stone in its path. Nokama suddenly found herself flying across the room. She slammed into the far wall, stunned.

"Should not exist," repeated Gaaki. "But obviously does."

Inside the mask chamber, Krahka paused in her work to listen to the sounds of battle. She could recognize Nokama's voice and knew she might have only moments to finish her task. Still, the thought of flinging open the door and crushing the Toa of Water was very appealing. . . .

No, she told herself. Time enough for that later. Roodaka's plan will weaken the Toa, making them easy victims whenever I so choose. But Roodaka falls first.

She shapeshifted into the form of Vakama and stepped over to where the masks were stored. They were sorted into six slots, silver-gray Great and Noble masks just waiting for someone to don them and use their power. Above each slot was a hieroglyph representing one of the six elements, but that was not what concerned Krahka. No, she was more interested in what *wasn't* there.

According to Roodaka, a Ko-Matoran seer had made a special trip to the Great Temple shortly after the first appearance of the Morbuzakh plant in the city. He had carved names above each of the six slots, names of those Matoran destined to be Toa Metru. When this was discovered by Ga-Matoran, they had hastily filled in the carvings, preferring that the will of Mata Nui not be revealed in such a way. It was Krahka's job to bring those names to light again.

Using pinpoint control of heat and flame, she quickly melted away the protodermis used to fill in the carvings. One by one, the names reappeared. As she read them, Krahka could not stop a smile from playing across her lips.

Oh, yes, she thought. *Whatever else Roodaka may be, she is cunning. Too cunning to be allowed to survive.*

The sounds of battle grew louder from the other side of the door. Her work completed, it was time for Krahka to make her exit. Willing herself to transform, she shifted into a duplicate of a gaseous creature once encountered far beneath Onu-Metru. Then she slipped beneath the crack at the bottom of the door and drifted into the outer chamber.

Nokama was a little too busy to notice the mist that floated by just below the ceiling. Her efforts to go around and over the guardian had all met with failure. Without so much as touching her, it had been able to flatten her time after time. With each blow, her rage grew. She could feel her

Hordika side taking control, but she no longer cared.

Gaaki had hung back and watched the uneven conflict. There had to be an answer to what was happening here, and it had to be found while Nokama was still rational enough to listen to it. The Toa Metru of Water would have given up on charging headfirst long ago, but a Toa Hordika had little concept of strategy ... only savagery.

Nokama leapt. The guardian lashed out with a kick. The Toa Hordika dropped in mid-leap and slammed into the floor.

It's making the moves, but never making contact with her, thought Gaaki. *At least ... not that we can see.*

Gaaki waited until Nokama mounted another attack, then launched her Rhotuka spinner at a point several feet above the guardian's head. It wouldn't do any damage if it struck, but it might solve a mystery. The guardian never noticed it coming, being too busy knocking Nokama flat again. Gaaki's keen eyes followed the spinner as it flew straight and true, then seemed to strike an invisible wall. The spinner fell to the ground, its energy dissipating.

The Rahaga rushed over to where Nokama was trying to rise. "It's not what it looks like!" Gaaki said hurriedly. "That's the answer!"

Nokama shoved Gaaki aside with a snarl, but the Rahaga refused to back down. "Nokama, listen to me! Listen! All a Hordika knows is brute force, but brute force won't work here!"

"Then what will?" Nokama exploded. "Tell me!"

"Do you remember the cave fish? When it's threatened, it makes itself appear larger. This guardian does the opposite — it makes itself look smaller!"

Nokama struggled to comprehend what she was being told. It was difficult for the words to penetrate the haze of anger in her brain. "Smaller?"

"The guardian you see is mimicking the movements of the guardian you *don't* see," said

Gaaki. "It's projecting a miniature version of itself as a deception, while it strikes out at you."

Nokama nodded. "The real guardian is invisible . . . water could change that. If I still had my powers. . . ."

"You do," said Gaaki, helping Nokama get to her feet. "Your Rhotuka spinner, Toa. Concentrate and launch it!"

Nokama had tried not to think about the strange spinner and launcher that had become part of her body after her transformation into a Hordika. Now that she tried using it, she found it extremely difficult. It required more willpower than triggering elemental powers ever had before. Then, suddenly, it happened — a whirling sphere of energy flew from the launcher and shot across the room at the guardian.

An instant after it struck, a torrential rainstorm began inside the chamber. The drops formed an outline of the guardian's true shape, which was easily seven times the size of the miniature version. Nokama smiled, but there was no good humor in the expression. It was the smile of a predator on the hunt.

"Now let's see how good you are in bad weather," she said, hurling herself at the guardian.

The miniature guardian launched a vicious kick, a move duplicated by its far bigger true self. But now that Nokama could see her foe, she was able to dodge the blow, dive and roll. Striking the guardian's legs, she upended it. Like a felled tree, the creature toppled over and slammed into the opposite wall. Nokama sprang and pinned her enemy to the floor.

"I am a Toa," she growled. "I am! I am!"

"It's all right, Nokama. It's over," said Gaaki. "You've won."

Slowly, reason returned to Nokama's eyes as she forced her Hordika side down. She looked up at the Rahaga, ashamed. "I . . . I lost it, didn't I? I lost myself."

"But you got yourself back," said Gaaki. "That is what matters."

Nokama rose and opened the inner door leading to the mask chamber. She vanished inside.

An instant later, Gaaki heard her gasp. The Rahaga rushed in to find out what was the matter.

The Toa Hordika was staring at the wall of compartments holding the Kanohi masks. Carved above each slot was the name of the Matoran destined to wear these masks as Toa. Gaaki squinted to make out the one Nokama's eyes were locked upon.

It was inscribed beside the symbol of water, and it read: "Vhisola."

"Wrong name. Wrong, wrong, wrong."

Kualus was walking through the long central corridor of a Knowledge Tower, glancing at records and muttering to himself. Far ahead of him, Nuju was doing his best to ignore the Rahaga and focus on his mission. But it was growing increasingly difficult to shut out the constant stream of comments.

"Oh!" exclaimed Kualus. "No, no. Who thought of that?"

Nuju stopped in his tracks and turned around, slowly. He glared at Kualus. The Rahaga was looking at a collection of carvings relating to Rahi, all of which were on loan from the Archives. "What is it?"

"Gukko? What kind of a name is Gukko?" replied Kualus, as much as to himself as to Nuju.

"That is what that species of bird is called. That is what it has always been called."

"Well, it's not what they call themselves, I can tell you that," said Kualus. "The word 'Gukko' might even be an insult in their language. I don't know, I would have to ask."

"Some other time," said Nuju flatly. "We have work to do."

"Always so focused on the task at hand," said Kualus, walking quickly to catch up to the Toa Hordika. "How admirable. Why, I'll bet the air could be filled with flying creatures of all kind and you would never notice."

"If they made as much noise as you do, I would," Nuju said under his breath.

The Toa Hordika led his companion into the heart of the Knowledge Tower. Before them was a vast junction of transport chutes, as big as any in the city. Protected by the walls of the tower, these chutes had survived the quake largely intact. Though the exteriors were frosted over, Nuju could make out the movement of the liquid protodermis within.

Nuju walked to a niche in the wall and pulled out a long, curved blade that seemed to pulsate with energy. "All right. This is simple. Le-Matoran do it all the time." He handed the blade to Kualus. "Get up on top of the chutes and slice one in two places about 1.5 bios apart. As it falls, I will use my Rhotuka spinners to freeze both ends and seal in the liquid protodermis. But first —"

The Toa Hordika launched three wheels of energy, sending them curving beneath the tangle of chutes. The result was an ice ramp that would allow falling chute sections to roll safely near where Nuju and Kualus stood.

The Rahaga looked from Nuju to the blade and back to the Toa again. "Why?"

"Propulsion," answered Nuju. "The proto-dermis builds up tremendous force in the chutes.

By fitting the sections into an airship, and then creating a small opening in the ice covering the rear of the chute, that force will propel us forward."

Kualus looked doubtful, but he dutifully bounded to the top of one of the chutes and raised the blade. With a final glance at Nuju, he brought it down, slicing into the magnetic field that lined the transport tube.

Suukorak exploded from inside the chute, knocking Kualus off balance. The Rahaga fell, barely catching the blade into the underside of one of the tubes and hanging on for dear life. The horde launched multiple spinners at Nuju, trapping the Toa Hordika inside an electrical force field. Assailed by bolts of lightning and unable to move, he could only watch as the Visorak spiders turned their attentions to the Rahaga. Nuju closed his eyes and waited for the screams to start.

5

"Where is it? I know I saw it here last time." Whenua was rummaging through an Archive storage room, tossing priceless artifacts this way and that as he searched. Bomonga watched in silence. He had no idea what the Toa Hordika was looking for, nor did he care enough to ask.

With a cry of triumph, Whenua pulled a fragment of an ancient tablet from the pile. He blew the dust off it and proudly displayed it to the Rahaga. "This is where I first saw the name Visorak," he said. "It was brought to Metru Nui by traders long ago. It might contain information we can use."

Bomonga nodded. Reminding Whenua of the importance of knowledge had been wise. It had kept the archivist connected to the Toa Metru and the Matoran he used to be, vital if he was to resist the lure of his Hordika nature.

"No one knows where the Visorak came from or why," Whenua read. "Those few who have mastered their language claim that Visorak means 'stealers of life' and others say it means 'poisonous scourge.' Either way, no truer words have been spoken. Fear them, for they are a plague upon the land, leaving nothing but pain and fear behind them."

Whenua shook his head and peered closely at the tablet. "This next part is too worn to read . . . but the next . . . evidently, some Visorak Roporak tried to rebel against the horde rulers, Roodaka and Sidorak, and Roodaka . . ."

The Toa Hordika abruptly stopped reading. After a few moments, Bomonga said, "She killed them?"

"No," replied Whenua. "That would have been merciful by comparison."

Bomonga decided it was best not to let Whenua dwell on whatever he had read. "Let's get what we came for," said the Rahaga. "Time is short."

"What? Oh. Sure," answered Whenua, stowing the tablet in his pack.

It was an easy matter finding an armful of *increase weight* Kanoka disks in the Archives. These would be fitted into the airships along with *levitation* disks to make it possible for the vessels to take off and land. Once Whenua had them safely tucked away, he and Bomonga made their way toward an exit. Surprisingly, they were traveling farther down rather than up toward the surface.

"Might be faster to go through the lower levels than try the streets," the Toa Hordika explained. "Just keep your eyes open."

"Always," answered Bomonga.

Whenua took the shortest route possible. Part of this was because, even with so many of the former inhabitants now free to roam the city, this was still a dangerous place. The other part was that the Archives made his Hordika half feel trapped, as if the walls were closing in. He needed to be outside where he could see the sky.

Toa and Rahaga suddenly stopped short. Sounds of battle were coming from up ahead. Whenua peered cautiously around the corner and saw a gray Rahkshi confronting a huge Visorak spider. The Rahkshi was faster and more agile, but the Visorak was easily able to block its blows.

"Kahgarak," whispered Bomonga. "That's bad."

"How bad?"

"Watch."

The Rahkshi made another effort to slip past its opponent, only to be batted away by one of the Kahgarak's powerful legs. At this point, the spider evidently became bored with the whole conflict. It launched its Rhotuka spinner at its foe. When the spinner struck, a field of shadow suddenly appeared around the startled Rahkshi. An instant later, the Rahkshi was gone, swallowed completely by the darkness.

Bomonga answered Whenua's unspoken question. "It's still there. Trapped in the dark. You can't see it — it can't see you. Or hear you. Or touch you. Or escape. Ever."

"Right," said Whenua. "Let's try another direction."

The two turned around and moved quietly back the way they came. They had gone only a few steps when a shape loomed out of the darkness before them. It was another Kahgarak, its eyes fixed on them, its spinner about to launch.

You were a Toa?" said Matau, dumbfounded. "But you're . . . you're . . ."

"Short? Ugly? A little too Rahkshi-like for comfort?" said Iruini. "You can say it. I've said the same to myself for ages, and worse."

"But how . . .?"

"Norik is the storyteller of the group, not me. I don't know, those fire types always seem to want to tell tales. Must be all that hot air around them all the time." Iruini did a back flip from a standing start and landed atop a pipe.

"Who did this to you? How long ago?" asked Matau.

Iruini smiled. He could tell what Matau was really thinking. The Toa Hordika was worried he was going to wind up looking like a Rahaga. *If he's not careful, he may wind up as something worse, but no point in telling him that,* thought Iruini. *He's barely hanging on as it is.*

"It's like this. We six fought a battle and won, or thought we did. We didn't realize that our enemy had friends who would want revenge. Kualus, Bomonga, Pouks, and Gaaki were ambushed and mutated. Norik and I weren't with them for . . . different reasons. He and I saved the others from dying, but not before we were mutated ourselves. And here we are, one big happy family of freaks."

"You didn't completely answer my question," said Matau.

Iruini swung from the pipe, did a somersault in midair, and landed on top of a piece of machinery. "That's right, you wanted to know who would be cruel and sadistic enough to do this to another living being . . . what kind of monster could take delight in the suffering of another. Well, she has seen you, Toa, even if you have not seen her yet. She's the one who made you Hordika."

The Rahaga stopped and stood still, his eyes fixed on the ground as memories flooded back to him. He remembered the freedom and power of being a Toa and the satisfaction that came with protecting others. He recalled how good it felt to know that nothing could stand in his way as he fought for right. Then the horrible memory intruded, as it always did, of the night something ended his days as a hero.

"Roodaka did this," he said quietly, never looking at Matau. "She did it, and she laughed. The others may be here to save Rahi from the Visorak or search for some creature from an old Matoran tale. Me? I'm here to make sure Roodaka never laughs again."

Matau was not sure what to say. He had been so occupied dealing with what he had become and worrying about how to reverse it that he had not stopped to ponder vengeance. But he supposed that if you were condemned to a lifetime of living like the Rahaga, there might be little else to think about.

The Toa Hordika was about to end the awkward moment by suggesting they get on with their search, when Iruini held up a hand. Then the Rahaga dashed off toward the door. By the time Matau reached there, Iruini had shut it tight and was piling rubble in front of it.

"They're coming," he said. "Help me block this door."

Matau didn't need to ask who he was referring to. He could already hear the Visorak scratching on the outside of the door. It sounded like dozens.

"Are there other ways in?" asked Iruini.

"Windows, but they are tight-locked," said Matau, struggling to think. The nearness of the Visorak was making his Hordika side want to flee. "The . . . the hangar doors on the roof . . . if they were damaged by the quake, they could be open."

Without waiting for the Rahaga, Matau ran up the stairs that led to the roof. Along the way, he glanced out the windows to see Visorak crawling up the side of the building. The undersides of their bodies glowed grotesquely in the light of his torch as they passed over the panes. If they reached the roof first, he would never be able to shut the hangar doors in time to keep them out.

The sound of crystal smashing came from up ahead. One of the Visorak had thrust its leg through a window and was groping for the lock. Matau picked up a piece of pipe and struck at the spider, forcing its limb back outside. He could hear the scraping of spider legs through the walls. *Death by big bug is not the way for a Toa-hero to go,* he thought. *Even one who looks like I do.*

He looked up. Starlight was spilling through the hangar doors. They were wedged open by debris. A moment later, the stars were obscured by the bodies of Visorak as they gathered on the roof.

This will make a very dark-bad Chronicle, Matau said to himself. *If anyone is left alive to write it, that is. . . .*

* * *

Pouks looked up at Onewa. The Toa Hordika was shaking, not from the weight of the stone he carried, but from the war going on within him.

"There is always another way," Pouks said, pointing to the rock wall on the other side of the canyon. "All you have to do is look for it."

Onewa glanced in the direction the Rahaga was pointing. There was a cave mouth high up on the side of the wall. It was not a natural cave, rather the mouth had been carved out, with the edges in a distinctively jagged shape. Onewa smiled and hurled the boulder across the canyon and directly into that cave.

A response was not long in coming. Three rock raptors emerged from the cavern, looking about for who had dared to attack them. These bizarre looking Rahi made their home in Po-Metru and hunted creatures far larger than they. Their arms, each tipped with a blade for carving, waved in the air as they scanned the area. Their eyes rapidly fixed on the herd of Kikanalo far below.

The Rahi immediately went to work. They swarmed over the rock wall, chipping away at the stone. In a matter of seconds, the entire face of the slope was loosened. The stone slid down and crashed beside the herd, panicking them. As they scattered, the rock raptors dropped from above and went after the slowest of the beasts. Soon the entire canyon was deserted.

"See?" said Pouks. "Sometimes you charge like a Kikanalo, and sometimes you sneak like a stone rat. They both work."

"We better get down there before the raptors come back," Onewa replied. "They don't normally bother Toa or Matoran, but I don't look much like either . . . and neither do you."

The Toa Hordika and Rahaga scrambled down the slope. Their destination was a cave in which Po-Metru Kanoka disks were stored. Onewa had no doubt there would be some *levitation* disks in there, which were vital to constructing airships. Once they had those, they could return to Le-Metru and meet the others.

Onewa led the way. The disks were right where he remembered they would be. He had begun gathering them when he heard the sounds of crumbling rock from further in the tunnel. "Stay here," he said to Pouks as he went to investigate.

"Hold on —"

"Stay here, I said!" Onewa snapped. "If there's something back there . . . well, one of us has to get these disks back to the others."

The Toa Hordika moved cautiously down the tunnel. At one point, a stone snake slithered toward him, a good six feet long and powerful enough to crush rock in its coils. Ordinarily, this would have been a problem. But the snake seemed as disturbed by the Hordika as Onewa was by it and made a quick exit.

The source of the noise was easy to spot. An entire section of tunnel wall had collapsed, revealing a cavern beyond. It wasn't until Onewa stepped through the hole that he realized it was a chamber carved out of the rock. His Rahi side sensed danger. It took more willpower than he thought he possessed to keep from fleeing.

Even with the enhanced senses of a Hordika, it was hard to see. He reached out for the wall. His hand passed over a series of carvings, made relatively recently by the feel of them. Onewa ran both hands over them, trying to make out what they represented.

A chill ran through him. The carvings were a formula of sorts, the kind of thing Ko-Matoran in Knowledge Towers might study. He wished Nuju were here to interpret this. He wished almost anyone else was here in place of himself.

Twin suns . . . a time of shadow . . . the Great Spirit trapped in slumber . . . the universe gone dark. Onewa jerked his hand away from the carvings as if he had been burned. Suddenly, he knew what this place was, and who it had belonged to.

This was one of Makuta's lairs, he thought. *This was where he calculated when the suns would go dark and planned his crime against the Matoran. No wonder my Hordika side is raging inside me. It senses the evil that was done here.*

Onewa turned to leave and stumbled. He bent down to discover a tablet lying on the floor. It was too dark to tell what was written on it, so he picked it up and carried it out with him.

Perhaps it will contain some valuable information, he hoped. *A key to reversing this transformation or finding this Keetongu the Rahaga spoke of. Something, anything, to change our destiny!*

At the mouth of the cave, Pouks watched the stone snake slither by, winding its way rapidly into the mountains. Serpents were not his specialty — that was Norik's domain — but something about that creature just didn't *feel* right.

He glanced behind, but Onewa was nowhere in sight. If he was correct, there was no time to waste trying to find the Toa Hordika. He would have to do this job himself.

Pouks readied a spinner and set off after the stone snake. *If I catch it, maybe I can find out what it is that's disturbing me,* he reasoned. *And if it catches me . . .*

He decided it was best to not even think about that.

"Pouks, I found —"

Onewa stopped short. The Rahaga was

gone. He looked around, but there was no sign of a struggle or any trail. Half Rahi he might be, but a skilled tracker Onewa was not.

He looked at the tablet and began to read. After a few moments, the experience began to remind him of the time he had fallen into a troller nest. The sand and slime had clung to him and little by little he began to sink into the morass. He thought he would never escape . . . and he knew that, even if he did get away, he would never feel clean again.

His eyes fixed on one sentence. He read it over again, then a third and a fourth time. He kept hoping the words would change, but they didn't. Suddenly, everything made sense to Onewa, and at the same time nothing did at all. He only knew one thing: he had to get this to the other Toa.

They have to know the truth, he said to himself, *even though it will destroy us all.*

Vakama knocked the door down with one kick and stalked inside, Norik right behind him.

"You can't do this," the Rahaga insisted. "You're dishonoring his memory!"

"His memory? What about my life?" Vakama snarled. "I gave up everything — my home, my job, my friends — because I was chosen to be a Toa. If it was all a lie, I have a right to know!"

"But to break into Toa Lhikan's chambers . . ."

"He won't care. He's dead," replied Vakama. "Or didn't you know that? He died because he picked the wrong Matoran to be a Toa Metru."

A large cabinet stood in a corner of the simple room the late Toa Lhikan had called home. It was locked. Vakama raised a fist and smashed the cabinet into shards. A single tablet fell to the ground.

"You don't know that!" insisted Norik. "Maybe this is all some misunderstanding. "Are you going to abandon your friends, forget about saving the Matoran, all because of this? What if you're wrong?"

"I'm not," Vakama answered, tossing the tablet to Norik. The Rahaga barely caught it. "Read it. It's all there."

Norik scanned the stone. It had been written by Lhikan not long before his capture by the Dark Hunters. It read:

I am more convinced than ever that something is wrong with Turaga Dume. But if I am right, what can I do? I am one Toa against a Turaga and an army of Vahki . . . not to mention Nidhiki, who I am sure I spotted in the city the other day. I must have help!

But who? Who is worthy of becoming a Toa Metru? Logic would dictate it would be the six Matoran who discovered the location of the Great Disks. Surely that is a sign from Mata Nui! But when

I awoke this morning, I realized it was perhaps too obvious an omen, meant to divert me from the ones truly destined to be Toa. Vakama . . . Onewa . . . Whenua . . . Nuju . . . Nokama . . . Matau . . . those are the ones my heart tells me are to be the Toa Metru. They are the ones I must rely on to save the city.

Norik put down the tablet and looked at Vakama. "This proves nothing, other than that he had a change of mind."

"It proves he knew," replied the Toa Hordika. "He knew who the correct Matoran were, and something . . . or someone . . . changed his mind and made him choose us. I am going to find out —"

Norik ran out of the room before Vakama could finish. The Toa followed him. Outside, the Rahaga pointed at the webs overhead. Hundreds of Visorak spiders were traveling across the thin strands, all going in the same direction.

"They are on the move," said Norik. "And heading for Le-Metru. You know what that means?"

Vakama nodded. "It means Matau should have stuck to Ussal riding."

"I could use some help here!"

Nuju opened his eyes. Through the nimbus of electricity, he could see Kualus hanging by one arm from the bottom of the chute while he frantically beat back Visorak with his staff. But there were too many and the Rahaga was obviously tiring. It was only a matter of time before he fell, or worse.

The Toa Hordika reached out, only to be jolted by the electrical field that surrounded him. As long as it was in place, there was no way he could aid Kualus. When the Suukorak were done with the Rahaga, they would come for him.

No! I have the power of a beast now, he reminded himself. *I have the mind of a Toa to let me channel that power. I can — I will — make it through this barrier!*

Nuju lunged forward, hurling himself through the field. It felt like a thousand white-hot needles being jammed into his body. He screamed as the voltage slammed into him again and again. The Hordika side of him panicked and wanted to retreat, but it was his intelligence that dominated. Inch by agonizing inch, he forced himself through the field. When he finally emerged on the other side, he was drained and exhausted. But the Visorak would give him no time to rest.

The spider creatures had spotted him. A half dozen electrified spinners flew at him, but Nuju somehow managed to dodge them all. He responded with a flurry of spinners of his own, all of them carrying his elemental ice power. Wherever they struck, Visorak froze over.

He was fighting a losing battle, and he knew it. For every Visorak he stopped and every one driven back by Kualus, a hundred more took their place. It was going to take a miracle to survive this, and all he was getting was Kualus whistling and clicking and then whistling some more.

"What are you doing?" Nuju snapped, using his tools to fend off a Visorak. "This isn't the time to show off how you talk to Rahi!"

"Can you think of a better time?" Kualus

asked, smiling. The expression looked bizarre on a face that so closely resembled a monstrous Rahkshi. "I am just inviting some friends."

Tiny shrieks echoed then through the halls of the Knowledge Tower. Even recognizing what they had to mean, Nuju could not believe it. He shot a glance down the corridor and there they came, hundreds, thousands of ice bats. They poured into the chamber from every opening, hurling themselves at the Visorak, striking and then flying away. So thick were their numbers that the Toa Hordika could not even see his enemies anymore. He turned and almost bumped into Kualus who was now standing beside him.

"They will keep the Visorak busy and then retreat," said the Rahaga. "Something we should do as well."

"We need the chutes," said Nuju, still stunned by the chaos all around him. He had seen small groups of ice bats before, but never this many at once. The sight of them battling Visorak was so insane he wondered if perhaps he was really dead after all and this was all in his mind.

No, he decided. *I can't believe fate would be so cruel as to condemn me to an eternity with Kualus by my side.*

"We can get chutes elsewhere," said Kualus. "As much as I would love to stay and watch my pretty ones frustrate the Visorak, we have a date on top of this tower."

The Rahaga ran off, leaving Nuju no choice but to follow. He wanted to ask why they were running upstairs instead of down. If they were trapped on the roof by the Visorak, it would mean either capture or a very long and fatal fall to the street below.

Kualus burst through the roof door and immediately began babbling in his strange language. A few moments later, Nuju spotted two large Gukko birds soaring toward the Knowledge Tower.

"No, no," said the Toa Hordika, shaking his head. "I refuse to believe any of this."

The two birds landed on the rooftop. Kualus immediately climbed on top of one. Realizing the Visorak might well be on their way up, Nuju decided to escape now and argue later. He wrapped his arms around the Gukko's neck and just barely made it on top before the great bird took off.

"You haven't lived until you have flown one of these," said Kualus, happily.

Nuju glanced down at Ko-Metru, far below. "You haven't died, either."

The Rahaga laughed. "You see, Nuju, there is something to be said for speaking *to* Rahi, and not just *at* them. If the Onu-Matoran had learned that, they might have had less trouble in the Archives."

"I'll be sure to tell Whenua if I ever see him again," said Nuju.

"Now the next question is, which way should we go? Other than away from here?"

The Toa Hordika looked to the southeast. Hundreds of Visorak were crossing the webs, moving inexorably toward Le-Metru. "That way," he said, pointing toward Matau's home metru. "And let's hope we are in time."

* * *

Whenua ducked as the Kahgarak's spinner flew past and struck a display case. A moment later, the case and its contents were swallowed by the darkness.

The second giant spider was approaching from behind, trapping Toa Hordika and Rahaga between the two. Bomonga looked from one to the other, calculating whether he could get two spinners off before they attacked.

One of the Kahgarak launched again. Whenua shoved Bomonga out of the way as the wheel of energy flew at him. It narrowly missed the Toa, flying on to strike the second Kahgarak. It, too, was claimed by the darkness.

"I found our exit," said Whenua. "Let's use it."

Bomonga shook his head. "More that way. Launch a Rhotuka and catch it between your tools."

The command seemed strange to Whenua, but he did what he was told. As the spinner flew from his launcher, he caught the energy between his two Hordika tools. Instantly, he felt something like an electric shock go through his body. "W-what's happening?"

"Charging the spinner," said the Rahaga. "Makes it more powerful. Now let it go."

With an effort, Whenua disengaged his tools from the spinner. The energy flew downward and struck the floor. Its earth power unleashed, the spinner ripped open a massive chasm, sending Toa, Rahaga, and Kahgarak tumbling down.

"You were supposed to aim it!" shouted Bomonga.

Whenua grabbed onto the Rahaga's hand. "Hold on! There's water below and I think —"

The Toa Hordika didn't finish his sentence, at least not in the world he knew. The Kahgarak managed to get off a spinner even as it fell, striking Whenua. The darkness effect encompassed both Toa and Rahaga, plunging them into shadow.

"— we can hit it, and . . ." said Whenua. "Um . . . where are we?"

He looked around. They were no longer

falling. In fact, it felt as if they stood on solid ground. But all around was darkness. Only Bomonga was visible, and even he only dimly.

"Inside the dark," said the Rahaga. "Maybe forever."

"Oh, no," answered Whenua, the panic of a trapped animal creeping into his voice. "I won't be confined. I can't be. I need to be free to run, to climb, I need to —"

"Help your friends," reminded Bomonga. "Save the Matoran."

"Yes, of course. That too," said Whenua. "We have to find a way out!"

Something brushed against the Toa Hordika. He jumped. He couldn't see anything, but he could feel the presence of another creature and sense its movements in the ground. It was large, multi-legged, and walking away from them.

"The other Kahgarak!" he whispered. "It's here!"

Now Bomonga could sense it too. "Follow," he said. "Don't let go of me or you will never find your way out."

Toa and Rahaga moved cautiously through the pitch darkness, following the sounds of the Kahgarak up ahead. It reminded Whenua of trying to labor while wearing a blindfold, an exercise Turaga Lhikan had said would help him master his Toa powers. He had not been good at it, but there was much more than self-knowledge at stake now.

"Where are we going?"

"Where it's going."

"What if it's going nowhere?"

"Then we will have a new experience," said Bomonga.

"Oh good," muttered Whenua. "Mata Nui knows I haven't had any of *those* lately."

"Your slithering needs work," said Pouks, out of breath. He had trailed the stone snake halfway up the canyon wall. It had never turned back to look at him, but he was not so foolish as to believe he had trailed the creature undetected. More likely, it simply didn't think he was worth noticing.

Once he spoke up, the serpent twisted its

body and hissed at him. Pouks simply shrugged. "Now where I come from, the snakes know how to slither. Used to drive Norik crazy trying to catch them. You could learn something from them."

The stone snake shot forward and wrapped its coils around the Rahaga. Pouks made no effort to resist or escape. Instead, he looked almost bored. "You could learn something from me, too. Of course, you won't, not if you crush me to death. But go ahead, if you want to. Maybe Roodaka will even pat you on the head if you're good."

The stone snake's face suddenly twisted into an expression of rage. It kept on twisting, along with its body, until the serpent was gone, replaced by a perfect replica of Roodaka. Pouks looked the image of the Visorak viceroy up and down, saying, "Your power is amazing, even if I don't think much of your taste in subjects."

Krahka regarded Pouks through the eyes of Roodaka. "Why were you following me?"

"You're a Rahi," the Rahaga replied. "I hunt Rahi."

"And now you are hunted in return."

"We all are," said Pouks. "Anything that stands in Roodaka's way will end up in a cocoon, you and I included. Unless . . . you made a deal with her? Is that why you were sneaking around that cavern?"

"I am the last of my kind," Krahka replied. "I do what I must to survive."

Pouks snorted. "You are the last of your kind *here*, Rahi. But here is not the end of the universe."

Krahka grabbed Pouks and lifted him into the air. "Speak! Tell me where the rest of my kind can be found, or I will show you pain beyond even what Roodaka could inflict!"

"No need for that," Pouks said. "No need. I knew where others like you once lived. It was a green and peaceful place, until the Visorak came. Oh, your brothers held out the longest, but they too fell in time. The last I saw, they were trapped in a webbed tomb just like the Rahi of Metru Nui have been."

Krahka tossed him aside. Pouks struck

hard against a rock and lay still. "Roodaka promised me freedom in return for my service," the Rahi said. "I am not ready to challenge her again. I must follow her orders until I am ready. But . . ."

"That's right. Do what she says, Krahka."

The Rahi whirled to see Onewa standing on a ledge. The Toa Hordika smiled. The expression was a gruesome one on his bestial face. "Be a pawn. Be a tool. Be another soldier in Roodaka's army who always follows orders, no matter what. The last time we met, I thought you were a creature of pride and intelligence. But I guess you're just another dumb beast."

Krahka's mind flashed back to her first encounter with Onewa and his fellow Toa. They had invaded her home beneath the Archives, or so she had believed. Her efforts to oppose them met with failure, but she had vowed to return and challenge them another day. Now the Toa had fallen to someone else, but she felt no joy. Instead, she realized that a being powerful enough to mutate a Toa Metru could do infinitely worse to her and every other Rahi in the city.

The shapeshifter transformed into a squat, slime-caked creature with wicked blades for hands, something that made even a Hordika look good. "I have no love for Toa," she hissed. "Less for those pathetic Matoran you insist on protecting. This city should belong to me and my Rahi brothers! But . . . I cannot rule a ruin, and that is all Roodaka and her kind will leave behind."

Krahka's new form stretched itself to twice its height, a truly gruesome sight. Onewa never blinked or turned away. "So, you have a plan?" said Krahka.

The Toa Hordika glanced up. Visorak of all types were creeping across the webs, heading for Le-Metru. "No. But I think they do."

Krahka watched the spiders marching toward another conquest. From what she had heard during her time posing as one of them, she could guess where they were going. The Toa had little time left.

"Come," she said. "We have much to talk about, you and I, and a . . . friend to pick up along the way."

Onewa revived Pouks and together Toa, Rahaga, and Rahi moved off into the rocky passes of Po-Metru. Their attention was fixed on the small army of spiders ahead of them, so none noticed the Visorak Roporak appear as if by magic where they had been standing. Its color shifted from the sandy shade of the rocks back to its normal dark brown. There were times, it reflected, that being able to match perfectly any background and stand completely still for hours was a most useful talent indeed.

Effortlessly, it scaled a nearby web, but it did not follow the other Visorak. Instead, it veered southeast, heading for the Coliseum and Roodaka, with a most interesting tale to tell.

Matau reached the top of the staircase even as the first Visorak began pouring into the hangar. There was no time to make a plan. Instead, the Toa Hordika launched air spinner after air spinner, summoning hurricane winds to blow the spider creatures away. At the first opportunity, he wrenched the door shut and shoved a pipe through the handles to bar it. The Visorak immediately began pounding on the other side, denting the metal of the hatch.

Somewhere, another window shattered. Matau looked down and could not see Iruini. *This is very dark-bad,* he thought. *Too many open-ways to keep closed. We will never keep the Visorak out.*

"Matau! Help!"

The voice did not belong to the Rahaga. It was Nokama!

"Matau! Let me in! Please!"

The Toa Hordika raced down the stairs. The pleading voice was coming from the other side of the main doors. Nokama and Gaaki would be trapped out there among the Visorak.

"Hang on, Nokama! I will let you in!" he shouted, already pulling apart the barricade Iruini had erected.

"Hurry! They're everywhere! I—" Her words were cut off by a scream.

Matau was about to push aside the last pile of debris when Iruini slammed into him, knocking him off his feet. Though small, the Rahaga's strength was surprising as he managed to pin down the Toa Hordika.

"Don't open that door!" Iruini shouted.

"But Nokama—"

"Matau! Please! They're killing us!" Nokama pleaded from outside.

"That's not Nokama!" said Iruini. "It's a trick. If you open that door, we're as good as dead!"

"Matau! What are you waiting for?"

Nokama's words pierced Matau's heart. She

was a friend, and at times he wished she could be more than that. He could not leave her outside to die, no matter what the consequences. He knew her voice. It *was* her. *And why should I believe some Rahkshi-headed freak over my own instincts?* he asked himself.

Matau threw Iruini off and ran for the door. The Rahaga scrambled to his feet and went after him.

"Ask her something!" Iruini said. "Ask her something only she would know!"

Nokama screamed again. Matau pushed Iruini away. "This is no time for a quick quiz! She is dying!"

Matau tore away the last of the barricade. Ignoring Iruini's protests, the Toa Hordika undid the lock and flung the door open.

A dozen black Visorak stood on the other side. There was no sign of Nokama or Gaaki. The lead Visorak, Oohnorak, gnashed its teeth, but the voice it produced belonged to the Toa Hordika of Water.

"Thank you, Matau," said the Visorak in Nokama's tones. "We knew we could count on you."

At that moment, the real Nokama and Gaaki were crossing back into Le-Metru. They had successfully hidden the Masks of Power for loading on the airships later. Now they traveled through the waterways, breaking the surface occasionally to scout the area.

It was Nokama who first spotted the tower. It looked like a bad imitation of one of the Coliseum towers, but as she drew closer, she saw the truth was far worse. The tower was made of debris and Visorak webbing. Cocoons containing various Rahi hung all along the sides. At least a hundred Visorak of all types swarmed over the structure, reinforcing it. At the top of the tower stood a powerful crimson figure, obviously directing the horde. This was no Visorak — he stood on two legs and towered over the spiders, wrapped in an aura of command.

"Who is that? What is that?" whispered Nokama.

"The who is Sidorak, king of the Visorak hordes. He commands them in the field," said Gaaki. "A good tactician, brutal, his answer to everything is overwhelming force. That has worked well for him . . . so far."

"And that tower? I am no expert on Le-Metru, but that wasn't there before."

"The Visorak build them as bases," the Rahaga answered. "Staging areas for attacks. My guess is they know Matau and Iruini are here. They are planning a devastating strike to capture them both."

"This is a disaster," said Nokama.

"No," replied Gaaki. "This is an opportunity. You must learn to know the difference, Nokama."

Nuju and Kualus spotted the tower as well, from high above. Nuju immediately began urging his Gukko bird down toward a nearby rooftop. Kualus watched him, shaking his head.

"That's not a very good idea," said the Rahaga.

"Scouting out the enemy's location and gaining knowledge is always a good idea," said Nuju as his winged mount dove.

"I didn't mean that," Kualus yelled after him.

The Gukko came in for a perfect landing on the roof of an abandoned vehicle factory. As soon as Nuju had dismounted, the bird flew off again. The Toa Hordika looked around for the best vantage point from which to monitor the tower. Before he could find it, six Vahki Vohtarak suddenly appeared around him.

"That's what I meant," Kualus shouted from above. "Invisibility. I really hate that."

"Are you sure this is a good idea?" Onewa asked for the fourth time.

Krahka had led him to the edge of a massive hole in the center of Ta-Metru. Onewa had never seen the spot before, but Nokama and Matau had told him what had happened here. While searching for the missing Toa Lhikan, they and Vakama had encountered a rampaging monster called Tahtorak. Using *weakness* disks, they had succeeded in causing the pavement to give way beneath the beast, but not before it had destroyed a large section of the metru.

"Do you have a better one?" asked Krahka, transforming herself into a winged insect four feet in length. "We need allies against Roodaka."

"And we can't be too choosy about them," said Pouks.

Onewa looked down at the tablet in his hand. He had been wondering ever since he encountered Krahka in Po-Metru just how it was that he had so conveniently discovered Makuta's lair. For that matter, the tablet had been strangely easy to find as well.

"Speaking of proof," he began, "you planted this, didn't you?"

Krahka shrugged. "Yes. Roodaka wanted you to learn the truth about yourselves, for her own reasons. I was told to deliver it to you."

"Truth? What this says . . . this has to be a lie," insisted Onewa. "If it isn't . . ."

Krahka looked down from where she hovered in the air. "The only deception was in how you found it. The words are real, their meaning is real. That is why Roodaka considered it her ultimate tool against you."

"Well, she had that right," Onewa muttered as Krahka vanished down the hole. "When the others find out about this . . . even if we win, we lose."

Whenua and Bomonga had been following the Kahgarak for what felt like years. At one point, a noise to the right distracted the Toa Hordika and he almost lost sight of their quarry. Had Bomonga not grabbed his hand and pulled him ahead, Whenua might well have been completely lost in the darkness.

"How much farther?" he asked.

"No way to know," replied the Rahaga. "It may be lost, trying to find a way out."

"Just like us. And if it can't find an exit —"

"Then neither will we," said Bomonga. "Ever."

*   *   *

Roodaka sat on Makuta's throne, impatient. Sidorak had left some time ago to oversee operations in Le-Metru. By now, he should have returned with at least Matau and Iruini, if not the whole miserable group of Hordika and Rahaga.

Unless he has bungled it, she thought. *If that is the case, then Makuta will be displeased. Once the master of shadows is free again, Sidorak will be out of favor and I will rule by Makuta's side.*

She smiled. Ever since she and Sidorak had turned six Toa into wretched, twisted Rahaga, they have been competing with each other for Makuta's favor. So far, neither Sidorak's victories in the field nor Roodaka's subtle schemes had secured either one the role they coveted: command over all of Makuta's lieutenants. She knew that the battle for Metru Nui might be her last chance to seize power from Sidorak and secure the right to rule by Makuta's side. She was determined to succeed, even if she had to crush the king of the Visorak hordes in the process.

Her dreams of destruction were interrupted

by the approach of a single Visorak Roparak. She recognized it as the one she had ordered to keep watch on Krahka. The news it related came as no surprise.

"Of course, she betrayed me," said Roodaka. "It is just what I would have done. She is not as different from me as she would like to believe."

The Roparak continued its report, detailing how Onewa and Krahka had left together, apparently planning to follow the horde to Le-Metru. Sidorak had summoned Visorak from all over the city for a strike against a Toa and Rahaga hiding in a Matoran airship hangar. Even now they were assembling at the tower in Matau's district, waiting for the order to advance.

"As usual, Sidorak would topple a building to swat a fireflyer," said Roodaka. "But in this case, he may have blundered on to a plan. The movements of the horde will attract the attention of the other Toa Hordika. They will race to Le-Metru to save their friend, like flies hurrying into a web. And you know what happens when something is caught in our web, don't you?"

The Roparak nodded.

"Go to Le-Metru. Find Sidorak," Roodaka ordered. "Tell him to summon a Kahgarak and have it open a portal. The time has come to unleash the stalker in the shadows, the Zivon, once more."

The Visorak turned and fled the chamber. As it raced across the webs heading for Le-Metru, it could not suppress a shudder. In the past, the hordes had done many things that other species might view as monstrous or evil, and they had done them happily. But releasing the Zivon for any reason — that was beyond horror, beyond evil. That was madness.

It will surely mean the end of the Toa Hordika, thought the Roparak. *Let us hope it's not the end of the Visorak as well.*

Four Vahki Zadakh moved cautiously through the streets of Ta-Metru. They were far from the canyons of Po-Metru they normally patrolled, but the changes in Metru Nui meant every Vahki enforcer had to do its part to preserve order.

Their goal was the Coliseum. Metru Nui's tallest building soared high into the sky before them, though it lacked the grand appearance it once had. Now the facade was cracked and the entire structure was shrouded in webs. High levels of Visorak activity had been registered here. The Vahki's mission was to eliminate these creatures of disorder as a first step toward pacifying the entire city.

The patrol leader signaled for the rest to spread out. It had no doubt that these Rahi would fall easily to the power of the Vahki, but tactical programming suggested that approaching from multiple angles was practical. Once all four were in their proper position, the march resumed.

The Vahki on the far left flank was the first to encounter the target. A Visorak Boggarak crawled along a web leading from the Coliseum to one of the empty Ta-Metru forges. The Vahki raised its staff and unleashed a blast which knocked the Visorak off the web. The Boggarak scrambled to its feet and glared at the Vahki. A low hum filled the air.

The Vahki took another step and stumbled. It looked down and noted that its right leg was no longer functioning properly. Somehow, what had been a solid limb a moment before was now a rapidly dispersing gas. Worse, the effect was spreading across the Vahki's form. In a matter of seconds, it was no more than wisp of silvery gas floating in the air, its awareness dispersed over millions of molecules.

The Vahki on the right dropped down into four-legged mode, scaled a small building, and then climbed out on to a Visorak web. A quick scan revealed that there were no Visorak on this section. Traveling along the web would bring the Vahki right to what appeared to be a largely unguarded entrance to the Coliseum. Using its tools as forelegs, it began to crawl.

It had gone only a short distance when it realized that the amount of effort required to make it across the web seemed to be increasing. Energy use was up, mass had increased dramatically, and strangest of all, audio receptors were picking up a hum that had not been there before. The Vahki did a visual inspection of its structure, only to discover its outer surface was no longer gleaming metallic protodermis but solid stone.

The Po-Metru enforcer was pondering what could cause a Vahki to turn to rock when the webbing tore beneath it. The Zadakh plunged through the hole and hit the ground, smashing into hundreds of stony fragments. A Boggarak approached, kicked at the rubble that had been a Vahki moments before, and then crawled away.

The Vahki patrol leader paused. Several

Visorak were on the move between it and the nearest Coliseum entrance. The Zadakh turned to tell its second in command to wait until the creatures had passed before proceeding. But its lieutenant was not there.

Puzzled, the Vahki did a visual scan to all four points of the compass. There was no sign of any of the other three patrol units. The Zadakh took a step and then paused at a strange rustling sound from overhead. A glance up revealed its source: a Vahki cocooned in webbing, being carried across the webs toward the Coliseum by a pair of Visorak.

The patrol leader did a quick calculation. *Four Vahki departed on this mission. One remains,* it said to itself. *This will need to be reported. While success in this mission is vital, order can only be maintained if a strict accounting of the whereabouts of all Vahki is kept. New priority: prompt return to central hive.*

Naturally, it would not run. Vahki never ran unless in pursuit of a lawbreaker. Faced with the disappearance of three of its kind in a matter of seconds, though, the Zadakh was perfectly willing to walk very, very fast.

It glanced behind. No Visorak were following. That would look good in the report. The patrol had obviously scared the Visorak into staying out of Ta-Metru. That accomplishment might even mean elevation from patrol leader to squad leader.

Pale sunlight suddenly gave way to shadow. The ground shook. Believing it to be another earthquake, the Vahki seached for cover. It raced toward a large green and brown structure nearby.

A second tremor struck, then a third. The building rocked so hard it almost appeared to be moving. It was only after the Vahki was safely underneath the structure that it remembered there were no green and brown buildings in Ta-Metru.

The Vahki looked up, just in time to see the massive, clawed foot of the Tahtorak descending upon it. Then it didn't see anything else, ever again.

*   *   *

Forty feet above, on the Tahtorak's broad back, Onewa winced at the sound of Vahki being crushed. He was no fan of the order enforcers, but the more he saw of the Tahtorak, the more he was starting to think luring it back to the surface had been a mistake. It had already smashed half a dozen buildings to fragments and damaged countless more, and that was with Krahka directing its journey. What would happen if it went on a rampage?

One thing was certain — Onewa had never seen anything like this beast. When the Tahtorak climbed out of the hole, he was certain nothing could be that big. The Rahi regarded Onewa as if the Toa Hordika were a light snack. The Tahtorak's reptilian face was ringed by silver fins and his fierce jaws snapped in anticipation of a meal. His forelegs were surprisingly short, but the rest of his body was overwhelming huge and powerful. A single sweep of his tail was enough to turn a building into a pile of bricks.

"I want the answer!" the Tahtorak snarled. "Give it to me!"

"What is he talking about?" asked Pouks.

"I don't know," said Krahka. "That is all he would say when I found him down below. So I told him the Visorak have the answer, and they don't want him to know it."

Onewa shook his head, smiling. "If you weren't . . . what you are . . . you would have made an amazing Toa."

Krahka shifted her form to a perfect replica of Onewa, and said simply, "I know."

Nuju stood back to back with Kualus as the Visorak closed in. His ice spinners had managed to hold them off so far, but each one drained his energy that much more. He had already decided that if the Visorak began spitting web, he would grab Kualus and leap, counting on his spinners to form an ice slide beneath them. Any risk was worth taking to avoid being in those cocoons again.

The building shook beneath his feet. A few seconds later, it did it again. "Is this the Visorak's doing?" Nuju asked.

"I don't think so," Kualus answered. "They seem as disturbed as we are."

Nuju glanced past the ring of spider creatures. Now the source of the tremors was all too clear, not that the Toa Hordika believed it for a moment. After all, who ever heard of *two* Toa Onewa and a Rahaga riding a Rahi four stories high?

"I knew being a Toa would do this eventually," Nuju said quietly. "I have lost my mind."

Now the Visorak saw the newcomers as well. A few of them braced to launch spinners at the oncoming Rahi. Then the Tahtorak casually shrugged, bringing down two buildings and a major chute intersection in the process. That was enough to make the Visorak fall back, forgetting Nuju and finding more defensible positions on another rooftop.

"If you lost yours, mine went with it," said

Kualus, smiling. "A Tahtorak! Imagine! I never thought I would see one in the flesh!"

Seeing that the name meant nothing to Nuju, Kualus continued, "It's a predator from one of the lands south of Metru Nui. Down there, oh, there were whole packs of them filling the plains. Once they had eaten everything they chose to on one island, they would walk across the sea and start someplace else. But I can't imagine how one got this far north, or why it would be traveling alone."

The Tahtorak was upon them now. Nuju tried not to gag from the stench of its fetid breath. Both Onewas jumped off and landed on the roof, while Rahaga Pouks stayed on the Tahtorak.

"Just what Metru Nui needed," said Nuju. "Two of you."

One of the Onewas shifted into the form of Nuju. "Is this better?" the figure said in Nuju's own voice.

"For obvious reasons, I prefer to avoid

mirrors just now," the Toa Hordika replied. "I had hoped to avoid you as well, Krahka."

"I want the answer!" bellowed the Tahtorak, the sheer force of his yell almost blowing Toa Hordika and Rahaga alike off the rooftop.

"So do I," said Nuju. "A lot of them."

"Where are the others?"

"We saw Vakama, Norik, Nokama, and Gaaki heading this way from the air," said Kualus. "As for Matau and Iruini . . . no sign."

"They were supposed to be searching one of the hangars," said Nuju.

"I'm guessing that one," Onewa replied, pointing off in the distance. "The one the Visorak are pouring into."

"We will have to go get them, then."

"What?" snapped Krahka. "You are wasting time! Every moment you delay brings Roodaka and her horde closer to complete control of this city. What is one Toa more or less, compared to that?"

Onewa and Nuju said nothing in reply.

Using their spinners to form bridges of ice and stone, they hurried toward the hangars.

Kualus looked up at Krahka. "If you can't understand, then they can't explain it to you."

"Light!" Whenua shouted, pointing up ahead.

The Kahgarak paused for a moment before resuming its march. "Keep quiet," said Bomonga. "If it hears us and turns back . . ."

Whenua understood, but it was hard for him to curb his excitement. A pinprick of light had appeared up ahead in a world where all was dark. The Kahgarak was moving right toward it. Whenua felt certain it had to be an exit.

Bomonga was keeping a careful eye on the creature. If that point of light was a gate, it would vanish the instant the creature passed through it. They would have to go through right behind or risk never finding the point again. He watched as the light grew bigger and brighter, mentally count-ing down the seconds.

"Run!" he said abruptly, racing off to reach the Kahgarak. Taken by surprise, Whenua was a few steps behind. The creature reached the light and passed through. Bomonga and Whenua dove, barely making it through before the gateway disappeared.

They hit the pavement. Compared to the total darkness they have been traveling through, the brightness of this spot was like being hit by a fist. It took Whenua a long few moments to adjust to the glare so he could see again. Then he wished he had not bothered.

Toa Hordika and Rahaga were on the ground in Le-Metru. The Kahgarak was up ahead, standing beside a powerful, red-hued figure. Visorak were everywhere, swarming into and around a tower. As soon as the spiders noticed the new arrivals, they advanced to surround Whenua and Bomonga.

"How convenient," the figure exclaimed upon seeing the Toa Hordika. "You come to us, instead of us having to hunt you down. For that, you have the gratitude of Sidorak, king of the Visorak horde."

"A worthless gift," growled Bomonga.

Sidorak laughed. "Not at all. You two will be privileged to see the emergence of the Zivon into this city. It will no doubt be hungry after its journey. You two will make a fine meal, don't you think?"

Matau and Iruini retreated further into the hangar. All their efforts to stop the advance of the Visorak had failed. Every exit was blocked by the creatures as well. They both knew that, at best, they were delaying the inevitable.

"Any last words?" Matau said, throwing another piece of equipment at the horde.

"Yes," said Iruini. "Next time, keep the door shut."

Matau heard a crash behind him. He turned to see more Visorak coming toward them from the rear. They were trapped between two small armies of spider creatures.

"That mud-swamp on the island up above is looking better all the time," he said, launching an air spinner at the oncoming Visorak.

It never reached its destination. Instead, a second spinner flew down from above, striking the floor. A wall of fire suddenly sprang up, cutting off the Visorak. Matau looked up and saw Vakama and Norik standing at the top of the stairs.

Now chaos erupted in the hangar. Water, ice, fire and stone spinners were raining down on the Visorak. Battered by the sudden onslaught of elemental powers, the creatures retreated. Matau could guess why. Indoors, they were vulnerable to attack from too many hiding places. But with the Toa Hordika all in the hangar, the Visorak could go back to laying siege and eventually capture them.

Vakama, Nokama, Nuju, and Onewa assembled at Matau's side, while Norik and Gaaki secured the doors. "Not that I am not ever-happy to see you," said Matau, "but how did you get in?"

"I melted through the doors on the roof," Vakama replied, his voice hard. "I am — I *was* — the Toa of Fire. It's what I do."

"Unfortunately, you made an entrance for the Visorak that we can't close," said Iruini. "They will be back."

"I did what I had to do!" snapped Vakama. "I didn't see you coming up with any great ideas, Rahaga."

"There must be some way we can get out of here before they return," said Nokama. "Matau, is there a way out through the Archives?"

Before the Toa Hordika of Air could answer, a tremor shook the building. Then it rocked on its foundations as the roof was torn off, sending Visorak flying every which way. Startled, they looked up to see Pouks smiling down at them as the Tahtorak crushed the hangar roof to dust in his hands.

"Oh, good," said Nuju. "Our ride is here."

Bound with webbing, Whenua and Bomonga could only watch as the Kahgarak opened another gateway into the field of darkness. Visorak backed away, scurrying for cover. Whenua wished he could join them as the Zivon began to emerge.

It was gigantic, a horror so great the Toa Hordika had to make an effort to keep his sanity. Even in his days as an archivist, he had never seen such a thing. Towering over the nearby buildings, it looked like some obscene hybrid of a Visorak, an Ussal crab, and who knew what else. Its head was pure spider, but the twin claws that snapped buildings in two like dry twigs belonged to a sea creature. It moved about on six legs, its scorpion-like tail lashing out to level anything that caught its eye. Even Sidorak looked like he was questioning the wisdom of bringing this thing into the world.

The Visorak were keeping their distance, those that were not running away outright. One of the spiders made the mistake of running along a web too close to the Zivon. It snapped the unfortunate Visorak up in a claw and tossed it into its gaping jaws.

"Those fools," said Bomonga. "Those stupid fools."

"What is that thing?"

"No one knows its true name," said Bomonga. "It lives in the darkness we just passed through. It's not Visorak, but it has aided them in the past."

"Why?"

"It likes to keep its food source handy," the Rahaga replied. "The Zivon eats Visorak. It has been known to celebrate a victory by devouring half the horde it fought beside."

"Then why bring it here?" asked Whenua, shocked.

"Sidorak wants the Toa dead," Bomonga replied, "even if he has to destroy Metru Nui and everyone in it to make that happen."

High above, the Zivon's eyes narrowed at the sight of the helpless Toa Hordika and Rahaga. Saliva dripped from its mandibles, falling like rain on the Visorak tower, as it lumbered toward its next meal.

Vakama lifted his blazer claw and angled it to reflect the dim sunlight. On a nearby rooftop, Nokama did the same. One by one, the signal was repeated by all the Toa Hordika, relaying that they were in position for the strike.

"I am not sure I like this plan," said Nuju. "How are we supposed to take them by surprise with the Tahtorak wandering around?"

"The city is full of Rahi. He's just one more," replied Kualus. "Granted, a very big one."

It had only been a minute since Gaaki had reported seeing a monster emerge from out of nowhere to menace Whenua and Bomonga. All thoughts of waiting until dark or putting together a sophisticated plan had been scrapped then. If they did not move quickly, Whenua and the Rahaga were as good as dead.

Now the Toa were positioned about a block

away from the tower. Onewa was on the ground near the buildings closest to the Visorak base. High above, Krahka, in the form of the hunting falcon Nivawk, circled and looked for points of weakness. The Tahtorak, impatient, was rooting up chutes and throwing them into the sea.

Krahka/Nivawk screeched. It was a signal. Onewa unleashed his spinners at the ground, sending huge cracks running through the pavement. When they reached the already weakened buildings that ringed the tower, the cracks became chasms. One by one, the structures toppled over onto the assembled Visorak.

That was the signal for the rest of the Toa Hordika and Rahaga to go into action. All four remaining Toa launched their spinners into the cloud of dust and debris. Outnumbered as they were, their only hope was to sow confusion among the enemy.

The Zivon at first ignored the battle going on around it. After all, it really didn't care if the Visorak were killed — dead ones tasted just as good as live ones. Then a fire spinner struck it in the side, just painful enough to be annoying. Inches away from devouring Whenua and Bomonga, it turned to seek out the source of the attack.

"Lucky," said the Rahaga.

"You don't know this group of Toa," answered Whenua. "We make our own luck. Now let's get free of this webbing before that thing remembers we're here."

Onewa, Nokama, Matau, and Nuju were down off the rooftops now. They could hear Sidorak bellowing for the Visorak to regroup and advance. Barriers of ice, stone, and earth kept barring their way, cutting off small groups from rejoining the horde. Then the Rahaga would launch spinners into the knots of Visorak, further adding to the chaos. Up above, Vakama hurled weakened fire spinners designed to give off lots of smoke without much flame.

Krahka was the first to spot the Zivon moving toward the Toa Hordika of Fire. Used to living in darkness, the smoke and dust could not obscure the Zivon's vision. Krahka swooped down and dug her talons into the Tahtorak's flesh, spurring it on toward the Visorak's monstrous ally.

Vakama saw his danger too late. The Zivon's claw slashed toward him, only to be knocked aside by a sweeping blow from the Tahtorak's tail. Vakama leaped from the roof even as the Zivon charged, slamming into the Tahtorak's midsection and driving the beast back.

Nuju spotted Whenua trying desperately to free himself from the Visorak web. He launched a spinner and froze the webbing solid. A shrug was enough to shatter it then.

"This isn't the healthiest place to be right now," said the Toa Hordika of Ice.

"It was even less so a few moments ago," replied Whenua. "What's going on?"

Nuju gestured toward the tower, now being bombarded by air, stone, and water spinners. "We're giving the Visorak something to think about."

Bomonga watched as four Boggarak

tumbled off the tower and onto a web far below. "They won't forget this."

"Good. We don't want them to . . . let them remember, and fear."

On the far side of the tower, Onewa had forgotten the first rule of this operation. The spinners gave the Toa the chance to strike from long range. Closing in on the Visorak gave the spider creatures too many advantages. Caught up in the heat of the fight, Onewa had gotten too near. Now he was pinned against a wall with a half dozen Visorak moving in.

"All right, come on," he shouted. "Any Po-Matoran could take you! All they would need is a big enough stick!"

The Oohnorak launched their spinners. Onewa managed to dodge all but one, which struck his right arm, numbing it. The Visorak, sensing weakness, advanced.

"Okay, one arm," said Onewa. "I can beat you with one arm. Don't let how I look fool you — you're not fighting some dumb Rahi now. You're fighting a Toa!"

An Oohnorak leaped, crashing into Onewa and knocking him to the ground. Its mandibles grabbed the Toa's good arm while the Visorak closed in.

A short distance away, Matau was fending off the enemy with a long piece of pipe when he spotted Onewa disappear beneath a pile of spiders. An air spinner might blow Onewa away along with his attackers. Matau dodged a Roporak spinner and broke into a run. At just the right moment, he planted the end of the pipe into the ground and vaulted over the horde. At the apex of the vault, he let go, crashing feet first into the Oohnorak.

Before the Visorak could recover, Matau helped Onewa to his feet. "Thanks, brother," said the Toa Hordika of Stone.

"I couldn't let you go dark-sleep," Matau replied. "Who would there be for me to annoy?"

"I am sure you would find someone," said

Onewa. "What do you say we pay these monsters back a little of what we owe?"

Vakama landed hard and lay stunned. All around him, the other Toa Hordika were fighting for their lives. He knew he had to get up and help them. But something held him back. He had faced death, and worse, many times since becoming a Toa, yet never like this. Never before had he gone into battle with the knowledge that he was not meant to be a Toa . . . that this destiny belonged to someone else. And if it was not his destiny, then he might well die here, fate erasing a cosmic mistake.

He looked up. Through blurry eyes, he saw that the Visorak groups were starting to link up. In a few moments, the horde would be reassembled. Once that happened, the Toa and Rahaga would have no chance. They would fall, the Matoran would never awaken, and no one would be left to remember that Toa Metru had ever fought here.

And maybe it's better that way, he said to himself.

The Tahtorak smashed into a building. Krahka barely managed to avoid being thrown off. The Zivon's claws and mandibles were snapping at the Rahi's flesh, but hadn't yet been able to penetrate its scaly hide. Snarling, the Tahtorak reached down and grabbed the Zivon with his forelegs. Before his enemy could react, the Tahtorak had lifted it into the air and slammed it down onto its back.

But the Zivon was far from helpless. Webbing shot from the tips of its legs, tangling up the Tahtorak. Taking advantage of the distraction, it rolled over and got back to its feet, hissing and spitting venom.

Krahka shifted her form to that of a razor-fish and drove, slicing through the webbing on her way down. Just before she hit the ground, she transformed again, this time into an insectoid Nui-Rama. She flew straight for the Zivon's eyes.

Behind her, a very angry Tahtorak freed himself from the last of the web.

Flitting and buzzing around in the Zivon's line of sight, Krahka succeeded in distracting it. By the time it saw the Tahtorak's tail sweeping toward it, there was no time to do anything. The blow connected, sending the Zivon flying toward the tower.

From the top of the tower, Sidorak had been watching the struggle unfold. The Toa Hordika had taken his horde by surprise, that was true, but the momentum was already beginning to shift. Already, the Visorak were moving to isolate the Toa and Rahaga and finish them off. Barring the unforeseen, he would be sharing a victory celebration with Roodaka before the day was done.

A shadow passed over the sun. Sidorak looked up. At first, he wondered when the Zivon had developed the ability to fly. By the time he realized it hadn't, it was much too late.

*   *   *

Nuju and Whenua had fought their way over to join Nokama at the base of the tower. She did not look happy. "It's too big and too well made," she said. "And half the horde has retreated inside. I don't think we can take it."

"Maybe we're looking at this the wrong way," said Whenua. "Thinking too much like Toa. Try thinking like Hordika."

Nokama shuddered. "I would rather not, if it's all the same to you. I did that once already."

Nuju smiled. "No, he has a point. Tell me, archivist, what do Rahi hate the most?"

Whenua thought back to his years on the job, and then to the sensations he had experienced since becoming a Toa Hordika. The answer was easy. "Confinement. All wild things hate to be trapped."

"Exactly. The Visorak are trying to keep us from getting in the tower. What if we tried keeping them from getting *out?*"

Whenua's answer was cut off by an impact that shook the building. All three Toa looked up in time to see the monstrous form of the Zivon plunging toward them.

"Your friends need your help," said Norik.

Vakama looked down at the Rahaga. "They can do better without me. I am sure Matau or Onewa could tell you that."

"You are still angry about what you read in Lhikan's journal? Vakama, does it matter so much why you are a Toa, so long as you are one? You have the power — that gives you a responsibility to use it."

Vakama said nothing, but instead sprinted away toward Onewa and Matau. Norik wanted to see that as a success, but he could sense that something was happening inside of the Toa Hordika of Fire . . . something dark and danger-ous that, like an inferno, might well consume them all in time.

The impact of the Zivon striking the ground shook all of Le-Metru. Amazingly, the creature rose again, although it did stagger a bit in its first few steps. Krahka had shifted her shape once more, this time into a cousin of the Nui-Rama capable of hurling its stingers from a distance. She bore in on the Zivon, launching her barbs, only to see them bounce off its hard shell.

The Tahtorak, too, saw the enemy rise again. Ripping up the support struts of a chute, he threw them at the Zivon. The creature batted them away with its claws and charged.

The Kahgarak watched the Zivon mount its attack. The giant spider had been unconscious for part of the battle, so it had no idea where the massive lizard like Rahi or the flying insect creature had come from. But it certainly knew where they were going.

Spinner already energizing, it started after the Zivon.

Sidorak clung to the top of the tower. The nearest web was a long way below and there was no guarantee he would not simply plunge through it and end up a very messy blotch on the ground. Better to climb back up and reassess the situation.

A rumble came from below. He looked down to see a wall of earth rising up to surround the tower. At the same moment, water spinners produced a drenching rain centered on the structure. The ledge grew slick. Sidorak made a last effort to pull himself back to the roof, but his claws slipped. He hurled himself as far from the building as he could, aiming for what looked like a strong section of web.

The king of the horde struck the web like a rock, but the product of the Visorak held fast. He shook his head to clear it, then glanced at the tower. The earth now surrounded it, and ice spinners were turning the rain to sleet. Ice was building up on the soil, turning it into a wall as hard as stone surrounding the tower on every side. Every exit was blocked, with most of the horde trapped inside. Given time, they could force their way out again, he knew. Still, Sidorak had been leading the creatures a long time. He had seen what happened when Visorak were stuck in a confined space together. If he was lucky, there might be 50 or 60 left in the end out of the hundreds in there now.

Sidorak cursed in a language that had been old when Metru Nui was new. He knew this was only a temporary setback. He would return with another horde and free the tower in a matter of days. But now the Toa Hordika had seen that the horde was not invulnerable. They would not look at the Visorak with the same horror in their hearts again.

Then there is only one answer, he said to himself. *We must give them new reasons to fear.*

Vakama thought as fast as he ran. Turning the ground to tar beneath them would not stop the Visorak from launching spinners or shooting web. Fire bursts might slow them down, but not defeat them. A wall of fire would trap Onewa and Matau as surely as the spiders.

He was almost ready to give up in frustration when he noticed the overhang. The upper half of the building behind Onewa and Matau had been damaged in the quake, and it now hung out over where the Oohnorak were assembled.

For the first time in a while, Vakama smiled.

Onewa and Matau had watched the wall of earth and ice go up around the tower. It was an amazing sight — and possibly also the last one they would ever see. The Oohnorak were mounting charge after charge, barely held back by the stone and air spinners. Exhausted, neither Toa Hordika felt they could hold out much longer.

The lead Oohnorak sensed their weakness. The hunt was about to end. It took a step forward, another, and another. Then something struck its back, liquid, sizzling hot. The Visorak screeched and threw itself back.

Now a rain of molten hot protodermis had begun. Onewa and Matau watched in shock as the white-hot droplets poured down on the Visorak. Here was something they could not fight. A hastily woven web simply melted at the touch of the liquid.

Matau pointed upwards. Fire spinners were striking the overhang. It now glowed red and was rapidly melting. As he watched, one spinner went off course, striking further down the building. Fire spat from it, tearing through the weakened structure.

"Move!" yelled Matau, diving at Onewa. The two Toa Hordika barely managed to get clear as the upper part of the structure came crashing down.

"Are you all right?" Vakama was standing over them.

"Except for almost getting flat-crushed, sure," said Matau. "Your aim was a little off on that last one."

"A lot of things are off," said Vakama.

Onewa rose and helped Matau up. "More than you know, fire-spitter. More than you know."

"Give me the answer!" bellowed the Tahtorak. "Give it to me now!"

The only answer the Zivon gave was a slash with its claws. When the Tahtorak evaded, the

Zivon charged and grabbed its foe. Then its stinger began to strike, once, twice, three times, each time deeper than the last. The Tahtorak roared in pain.

Krahka dove for the ground, transforming into a Lohrak as she flew. She wrapped her snakelike body around the Zivon's stinger in a desperate attempt to hold it back. Spared from the blows for a moment, the Tahtorak tore off a portion of a nearby building and slammed it on top of his foe.

The Zivon reeled and snapped its stinger forward. Krahka lost her grip and flew into the Tahtorak. The Rahi batted her aside and she slammed into a wall. Masonry rained down upon her.

The Tahtorak reached the Zivon just as it sprang. They collided, toppling over, locked in a fierce struggle. The Tahtorak had strength and weight, but the claws, mandibles and stinger of the Zivon gave it multiple ways to hurt its foe. Seeing an opening, it struck with its stinger, looking to end the battle quickly. But this time the Tahtorak was ready. It caught the offending limb in an iron grip and, with a supreme effort of its powerful muscles, snapped the stinger off. The Zivon screamed and scrambled away.

On a pile of rubble nearby, the Kahgarak had seen enough. It sent its spinner flying through the air at the Tahtorak.

Stirring, Krahka saw the whirling wheel of energy heading for the Tahtorak. She knew what it meant. If the Tahtorak fell, then the Zivon would ravage all of Metru Nui, with nothing to stop it. Forcing herself to rise, she found she was too weak to fly. Instead, she summoned her memories of the six Toa Metru, her body taking on aspects of each of theirs.

There was no time to risk an elemental power blast, and her mind was too scattered to focus it anyway. Instead, she ran, harder and faster than she ever had before. She could already tell she would be too late. At the last split second, she veered off and hurled herself at the Zivon.

The spinner struck. The field of darkness opened to consume the Tahtorak, drawing the Rahi into eternal shadow. At that instant, Krahka struck the Zivon full force, driving it into the

Tahtorak. With all three in physical contact, the shadow swallowed them whole. In an instant, they were gone.

Onewa could not believe his eyes. With a howl of rage, he unleashed a stone spinner at Kahgarak. The massive creature turned in time to see it coming, but too late to stop it. A moment later, it was buried beneath a ton of stone.

The Toa Hordika stood for a long time, watching the rock dust settle. Pouks scrambled over the rubble to stand by his side.

"It's not much of a marker for her," said the Rahaga.

"Best I could do," said Onewa. "And more than she expected, I'd guess. I'm still not sure what happened."

"You six are Toa, dealing with the Rahi inside," Pouks replied. "Maybe she was a Rahi who discovered a little Toa inside."

10

The battle was over. Those Visorak still free had retreated to the border of Le-Metru until further orders. Now, days later, the Toa Hordika surveyed the field of victory and prepared for what was to come.

Onewa and Nuju had worked together to tear down the wall around the Visorak tower. It was hard work, made more so by the need to keep an eye out for spider creatures who might be waiting to leap out. When the last piece of ice and earth had been removed, they opened the hatch leading inside, ready for anything.

The first thing that struck the Toa Hordika was the stench. Visorak did not smell particularly good under normal circumstances. Trap them together for a few days and it was far worse. A rustle of spider legs was followed by the appearance of a dozen or so battered Boggarak. None of them seemed at all interested in a fight.

"Do we stop them?" asked Onewa.

"Instinct would say we should," Nuju replied. "But I am no longer sure I trust my instincts. They are no threat. It may be best to save our energies for the fresh hordes that will come against us."

The Toa Hordika spent most of the next day cleaning out the tower, chasing away surviving Visorak and burying the dead. When the ugly task was finished, they stood looking at the structure, puzzled.

"Now what?" asked Whenua. "Knock it down?"

"What purpose would that serve?" asked Norik.

"No purpose," said Vakama, looking hard at the Rahaga. "It just feels good."

"That's the beast talking," Pouks muttered. "Go ahead, think like Rahi. Act like Rahi. I could tell you stories about how many Rahi have escaped the Visorak over the years. They're really short stories."

"I think we can find another use for this," said Iruini. "That's if this pack of wild Muaka calling themselves Toa has the patience to do something worthwhile."

"Talk," said Nokama. "We'll listen."

Onewa hauled another piece of rubble toward the tower. It was backbreaking work, even with the enhanced strength of a Toa. As he walked, he remembered Iruini's words.

"We won this fight," the Rahaga had said. "We may win the next one, or we may not. You may take the Coliseum and free the Matoran . . . or free only a few and then be driven back. You need a place of safety to which you can retreat. This tower can be that place."

Onewa could remember his reply too. "You're crazy. I know something about stone. This tower is strong, sure, but eventually the horde would batter down the hatch and that would be the end of it. Even barricading it would only buy us a little extra time."

"Not if you use my idea of a barricade," the Rahaga had said, smiling.

Onewa came up over a pile of shattered stone to see the results of the Toa's labors. A new gateway had been constructed at the front of the tower. At Nokama's suggestion, it resembled a huge Kanohi mask, like the gates of the Coliseum. A strong portcullis had been put into place as well. The Toa Hordika of Stone paused to survey the structure, then shook his head and said, "Still not enough."

"Drop that and come here," said Iruini. "All of you, gather around."

The six Toa Hordika did as they were asked. Norik passed among them, gesturing for them to raise their tools and lightly touch the surface of the new structure. For an instant, their tools blazed to life, only to fade out again.

"What was that?" asked Nuju.

Iruini scampered away, picked up a rock,

and threw it at the portcullis. Just before it struck the bars, bolts of fire and ice shot from the walls of the gateway and disintegrated the rock.

"Just as your tools can charge your Rhotuka spinners with greater elemental power," said Norik, "you can charge other physical objects as well. You will have to repeat it numerous times to maintain the charge, but while it has a portion of your power, it will be a formidable barrier."

"Let's invite some Visorak to be our home-guests," said Matau. "I want to try this out."

"You'll find out, Toa, that the Visorak have a very bad habit," said Kualus. "They never wait for an invitation to come calling."

Roodaka stood on a rocky crag overlooking the protodermis sea. Here on the Great Barrier, she could view the entire city, enjoying the sight of it slowly being strangled by Visorak webs. She often came to this spot when she needed time to plan, far away from Sidorak's ranting.

Of course, that was not the only reason

she journeyed here atop a mutated Nui-Kopen wasp. The true attraction was a slab of protodermis marked with a Toa seal. Behind this slab lay imprisoned the master of shadows, Makuta. Her power, Sidorak's power, even the might of the assembled hordes was not enough to free her sovereign.

But the Toa have the power, she thought. *What they created, they can undo. And undo it they shall, if I have to rip the Toa power out of them.*

Sidorak didn't understand. To him, Metru Nui was just one more game of conquest. He hated the Toa Hordika because they were not surrendering before his might. Their resistance might serve to embolden the Visorak to rebel. In addition he knew that by now the Rahaga would have spun their wild tales of Keetongu, the Rahi said to have the power to undo everything Sidorak had built. If such a creature existed, and if the Toa found it . . .

"Nonsense!" she spat. "It is an old Rahaga's tale they have told for decades, trying to keep their wretched spirits up. There is no Keetongu. There never was. And even if it existed . . . I know how to deal with Rahi."

Roodaka turned and peered at the crystalline protodermis shell, trying to glimpse Makuta's face. All she could make out was a dark blur, but it was enough. She knew he was in there. She knew his mind was aware of her presence, even if his body could not move.

"Soon, Makuta," she whispered. "I have used the most devastating tool I could imagine against the Toa: the truth. Already, it must be eating away at their resolve. They will fracture . . . their spirits will crumble to dust . . . and in their last moments, they will know their return to Metru Nui served only to free their greatest enemy."

Makuta did not answer. But the shadows grew deeper around Roodaka, as if their master was offering a sign of his approval.

The Toa Hordika and Rahaga sat in a clearing near their newly christened "Tower of Toa." Vakama had used his Rhotuka spinner to start a fire. The Toa Hordika didn't really need the warmth — in fact, the fire put off their Rahi sides — but the Rahaga were not quite so immune to the elements. Despite their successes, the mood around the flames was grim.

"We did well," said Nokama, "considering."

"Considering what?" asked Matau.

Vakama glanced at the Toa Hordika of Water. He knew the answer to his question before he asked. "You learned the truth as well?"

"Yes," she replied. "We were never meant to be Toa Metru. The destiny belonged to others. But I suppose it is our destiny now, for good or ill."

"Lhikan knew," said Vakama, frowning. "But he went against his instincts. Something made him choose us. Why?"

Onewa rose. "I think I can answer that. But you won't like what you hear."

When none of the Toa responded, he continued. "Think back. Toa Lhikan suspected something was wrong in the city. Makuta, in the guise of Dume, sent the Dark Hunters to stop him. But the false Dume couldn't be sure they would succeed before Lhikan was able to create more Toa.

"So Makuta studied the signs in the stars. He discovered that the Matoran who had found the Great Disks were destined to be Toa. They were far from perfect candidates, but with Lhikan to lead them, they might have been an effective team. I guess he never considered that Lhikan might have to sacrifice all his Toa power to create a new team."

Matau wished he could find some way to drown out Onewa's voice. He could guess what was coming next.

"Makuta planted the thought in Lhikan's mind to choose other Matoran. Without his even being aware, Lhikan was being directed toward picking six strong-willed, stubborn types who would never get along, let alone follow any leader or be able to function as a team. In other words, us."

"It cannot be," whispered Nuju.

"I found Makuta's lair in Po-Metru," said Onewa. "I read the story in his own words. We are Toa Metru, brothers and sister . . . by the grace of Makuta."

"Born from shadows to defend the light," Vakama said quietly. "Is it any wonder the beasts inside us are so strong?"

"So what do we do now?" said Whenua. "Now that we know where we came from?"

Nokama looked at each Toa Hordika in turn. "We worry about where we're going . . . not where we've been. Makuta wanted us to turn on each other, fight among ourselves, so that he could succeed. But we stopped him. And we will go on stopping him and others like him. It's who we are — it's what we do."

The other Toa nodded their agreement. But in their hearts, doubts grew where none had ever been before, and the coming dawn felt very, very far away.

Epilogue

Silence reigned for a long time after Vakama finished speaking. When it was broken, it was in a most unexpected fashion. Tahu began to laugh.

"A . . . a grand joke, Turaga," he said. "Toa owing their power to Makuta . . . a wonderful tale, but surely not one meant to be taken seriously."

Vakama looked up at the Toa Nuva of Fire. In that instant, Hahli could swear she saw the rage of the Toa Hordika in his eyes. "This is not a jest, Tahu. This is deadly serious. Even you, who have faced Bohrok and Rahkshi, cannot know what it is to have your very spirit turned against you." The Turaga dropped his gaze. His voice grew quiet. "But I know. Mata Nui, how I know."

"Then all of that, everything you and Onewa learned — it was the truth?" asked Nokama.

"It was . . . a truth," Vakama replied. "But there was more, and worse . . . much worse . . . to come."

"Whatever your origins, Turaga, you wore the mantle of Toa with honor," offered Kopaka. "You lived by the three Matoran virtues: unity, duty, and destiny, in all that you did. Despite your differences, you stood beside each other and faced every menace as a team."

Now it was Vakama's turn to laugh — a long, cold laugh that would haunt the Toa Nuva in their dreams. "There is more to tell," said the Turaga. "Much more, but it must wait for another night. The stars shine too brightly on this evening, and the fire brings too much warmth. This story is one that must be told on a night as dark as Makuta's heart, when the cold grips your bones like Zivon's claws. We will wait for such a night . . . and then we will continue."

The Toa Nuva watched him depart, hearing his final words in their mind. *We will continue . . .* was it a promise, they wondered. Or was it a threat?